Maggie pulled the brush through her hair and brooded over the sheer contrariness of the man she was more or less married to. After kissing her silly that first night, then teasing and tantalizing her the next day, Luke had either lost interest or suffered a pang of conscience. He hadn't touched her since.

How could a woman let a man know she wanted him when he treated the very idea of sex between them as a joke? Maggie tossed the brush on the bed. Hard.

Today they were driving to Dallas. She would sneak off to Victoria's Secret and buy a couple of sexy nightgowns. And just what did she do then? she asked herself as she left her room. Parade around the house in a few scraps of satin and lace and hope he'd be swept away by lust?

Maybe she should level with him. *By the way, Luke, I was hoping you could train me in something other than riding. Mind if we go to bed so you can make a woman out of me?*

Dear Reader,

Welcome to Silhouette Desire, where every month you can count on finding six passionate, powerful and provocative romances.

The fabulous Dixie Browning brings us November's MAN OF THE MONTH, *Rocky and the Senator's Daughter,* in which a heroine on the verge of scandal arouses the protective *and* sensual instincts of a man who knew her as a teenager. Then Leanne Banks launches her exciting Desire miniseries, THE ROYAL DUMONTS, with *Royal Dad,* the timeless story of a prince who falls in love with his son's American tutor.

The Bachelorette, Kate Little's lively contribution to our 20 AMBER COURT miniseries, features a wealthy businessman who buys a date with a "plain Jane" at a charity auction. The intriguing miniseries SECRETS! continues with *Sinclair's Surprise Baby,* Barbara McCauley's tale of a rugged bachelor with amnesia who's stunned to learn he's the father of a love child.

In *Luke's Promise* by Eileen Wilks, we meet the second TALL, DARK & ELIGIBLE brother, a gorgeous rancher who tries to respect his wife-of-convenience's virtue, while *she* looks to *him* for lessons in lovemaking! And, finally, in Gail Dayton's delightful *Hide-and-Sheikh,* a lovely security specialist and a sexy sheikh play a game in which both lose their hearts…and win a future together.

So treat yourself to all six of these not-to-be-missed stories. You deserve the pleasure!

Enjoy,

Joan Marlow Golan

Joan Marlow Golan
Senior Editor, Silhouette Desire

Please address questions and book requests to:
Silhouette Reader Service
U.S.: 3010 Walden Ave., P.O. Box 1325, Buffalo, NY 14269
Canadian: P.O. Box 609, Fort Erie, Ont. L2A 5X3

Luke's Promise
EILEEN WILKS

Published by Silhouette Books

America's Publisher of Contemporary Romance

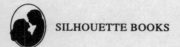 **SILHOUETTE BOOKS**

ISBN 0-373-76403-0

LUKE'S PROMISE

Copyright © 2001 by Eileen Wilks

Printed in U.S.A.

EILEEN WILKS

is a fifth-generation Texan. Her great-great-grandmother came to Texas in a covered wagon shortly after the end of the Civil War—excuse us, the War Between the States. But she's not a full-blooded Texan. Right after another war, her Texan father fell for a Yankee woman. This obviously mismatched pair proceeded to travel to nine cities in three countries in the first twenty years of their marriage. For the next twenty years they stayed put, back home in Texas again—and still together.

Eileen figures her professional career matches her nomadic upbringing, since she's tried everything from drafting to a brief stint as a ranch hand—raising two children and any number of cats and dogs along the way. Not until she started writing did she "stay put," because that's when she knew she'd come home. Readers can write to her at P.O. Box 4612, Midland, TX 79704-4612.

My heartfelt thanks to Mary Casper
for her invaluable assistance about the stabling and
training of horses for three-day eventing. Chances are,
whatever I got right is due to her input. Thanks, Mary.

One

Damned if he was going to let his brother get away with this.

Luke slammed the door to his Dodge Ram hard enough to loosen the hinges and sprinted up the steps of the big old house. He didn't press the doorbell tucked inside the gargoyle's mouth. Jacob always insisted this was still his brothers' house as much as it was his, though Luke and Michael didn't live there anymore.

After today, Luke's big brother just might reconsider his open-door policy. He jammed his key into the lock and swung the door open.

It was noon, lunchtime for most people. But Luke headed for Jacob's office, not the kitchen or dining room, betting that's where he'd find his quarry. Jacob would be doing what he did best—making deals, making money.

Luke shoved the door open so hard it bounced off the wall. "Good. You're alone."

His brother's only reaction was to look up from the papers stacked in tidy piles on his desk, his expression remote. "Yes. Sonia's in Georgia, cooing over her new grandbaby. And my new assistant doesn't start until tomorrow."

"I just bought Fine Dandy."

Jacob's left eyebrow lifted. "Maggie's horse?"

"You know damned well it is." Luke paced over to the desk, planted his hands on it, and leaned forward. "I thought you'd be *good* for her. All this time you've been seeing her, I thought—but you let her sonofabitching father put her horse up for sale!"

"Wait a minute. If you're talking about Maggie Stewart—"

"Of course I'm talking about Maggie Stewart!" Luke turned and paced the length of the office in several quick steps. "Are you telling me you didn't know about Fine Dandy? Maggie didn't tell you what her father was doing?"

Jacob shook his head.

Luke's breath gusted out. It looked like he'd built up a good head of steam over nothing. It wasn't the first time. He jammed his hands into his back pockets. "You can buy him off me, then, I guess. My head groom should be picking him up right about now...you can board him with me until Maggie decides what she wants to do." When Jacob's eyebrow lifted, he added irritably. "Quit with the Mr. Spock look."

"You know my situation. Cash is tight right now with the Steller deal still up in the air, and it will be months before we're able to dissolve the trust. If Fine Dandy's purchase puts you in a bind I'll help as much as I can, but—"

"I don't need your help," Luke snapped. "Dandy should come from you, that's all. Since you're her fiancé." Luke hadn't said it out loud until that second. The words tasted even more foul than he'd expected.

"No."

"What do you mean, no? Don't you care what that horse means to her? Or are you more like her father than I thought—determined to mold her in some image of your own?"

"Luke." Jacob shook his head. "I won't ask you to sit. You're no better at being still now than when you were four. But if you'd stop interrupting, you might learn something. Of course I want Maggie to have her horse, to continue to compete, if that's what she wants. But I'm not her fiancé."

Luke stopped dead, every muscle tense with disbelief. "Two weeks ago, when we met to discuss Ada's situation, you said you were going to ask Maggie to marry you."

"She turned me down."

A peculiar tightness squeezed Luke. The acid that had eaten him for the past three months—ever since Jacob started seeing Maggie—dribbled out, burning as it went. Maggie didn't want Jacob? "That's hard to believe."

"Is that supposed to be a compliment?"

"No." Luke frowned. The problem wasn't what he'd thought; therefore, the solution would have to change, too.

"Why would Maggie's father sell her horse?" Jacob asked. "I had the impression Malcolm Stewart's main interest in his daughter lies in how many trophies she can bring home.''

''Because the man's a fool. I'll lay odds it has something to do with that damned trainer he hired. Walt Hitchcock doesn't think women should be allowed on the Olympic Team—or much of anywhere other than the kitchen and bedroom.''

''Why would Stewart hire him, then?''

''He's got the credentials,'' Luke admitted reluctantly. ''Former Olympic medalist. Bronze,'' he added with a faint sneer that, perhaps, a former Gold Medalist was entitled to. ''Eleven years ago.''

''Maggie's an excellent rider.''

''Yeah, she's damned good. Not ready for the Olympics, though.'' As always, Luke made his mind up in a flash. ''Listen, Jacob, I've got to go.''

''What about Fine Dandy?''

''I'll take care of Dandy. Maggie, too.'' He headed for the door.

''Luke! Dammit, wait a minute.'' Jacob was a big man, half a head taller than Luke and thirty pounds heavier, but he could move quickly when he wanted to. When Luke reached the front door, Jacob wasn't far behind. ''What do you mean, you'll take care of Maggie?''

But Luke moved fast, too. When he wanted to. He hit the front steps at a run. ''You're not going to marry her,'' he called as he climbed into his truck. ''So I guess I will.''

The pickup was already moving when he slammed the door.

12:10 p.m.

''Your father will be so upset.''

''Here's a news flash. *I'm* upset.'' Maggie crammed a

fistful of panties into the corner of the suitcase and sniffed. Other women cried, she thought glumly. Take her cousin Pamela. Pamela cried beautifully, her eyes turning bigger and bluer with every tear. Not Maggie. Her nose got red and runny, but her eyes stayed dry.

"He isn't going to like this. You know what he says about your poor impulse control."

"At least I won't be around to hear him say it." Which was the whole point of making her escape now, while Malcolm Stewart tended to the important things in life— making money, crushing opponents. By the time he returned from his business trip, Maggie would be somewhere else.

Anywhere other than here, in his house.

"It's so unpleasant when you and your father are at odds. Are you—are you angry with me, too?"

She looked up and sighed. "No." What would be the point?

Sharon Stewart was a pastel woman. Eyes, clothes, hair, complexion—all were muted, but not to the icy clarity of sherbets or the welcoming warmth of spring. No, everything about her was tastefully understated to the point of invisibility. Her face was round, like her daughter's, the skin soft and pale and pampered. Her eyes were uncertain. Always. Even now, those gentle blue eyes admitted no more than a faint, perplexed anxiety, as if all the more vivid emotions had been washed away.

But her hands clenched and unclenched on each other, the knuckles strong and white. Broad hands, so much like her daughter's. Peasant hands, according to Maggie's father.

"He'll think I should have stopped you," Sharon said anxiously.

"Oh, Mom." Impulsively Maggie moved closer, laying her hand over one of her mother's. She caught the faintest whiff of Chanel. For as long as she could remember, her mother had used Chanel—discreetly, just a dab behind her left ear. The scent conjured memories of childhood hugs at bedtime. "Tell you what. Why don't you run away from home with me? Then neither of us will have to worry about Father's temper."

Sharon looked blank. "If that's a joke, Margaret, it's in poor taste."

"Maggie, not Margaret." She sighed and pulled her hand back. "How many times have I asked you to call me Maggie?"

"Your grandmother considers that a particularly vulgar nickname."

"I'm not my grandmother." Although she bore the old harridan's given name, for her sins. "Never mind. Pass me my address book, would you?"

Sharon handed it to her, and she crammed it into the side pocket of her already-stuffed purse.

"Where will you go? You don't have any money."

"I have enough." Especially since she wouldn't have to pay for Fine Dandy's stabling, feed, vet bills... Maggie slammed the suitcase shut. She had to lean her full weight on it, then fumble with the catches with her left hand. The cast made it awkward. "I'll get a job."

There was no reason not to. Not anymore. Anger, dark and roiling, gave her good arm extra strength when she swung the suitcase off the bed.

"But do you think...that is, with the economy so uncertain..."

Maggie wanted to wince, so she grinned. "The Dallas economy is in fine shape. Don't worry. I may be lousy at keeping jobs, but I'm great at getting hired. I'll find something.''

''If you'd just wait until tomorrow…. If you'd just talk to your father when he gets home. He *is* going to get you another horse. Walt Hitchcock said—''

''I don't give a holy hoot what Walt said!'' She raked a hand through her short hair, striving for patience. ''Father hired Walt, so he thinks the man is perfect. I don't. Which is why Father sold Dandy—I wasn't following the orders of his chosen trainer, so I had to be forced into line.'' She remembered last night's grimly polite scene with a shudder. ''I don't want another horse. I want Fine Dandy.''

''Oh, honey.'' Her mother raised a tentative hand as if she might pat Maggie's shoulder, but didn't complete the gesture. ''That's not the way it happened. You were hurt, and your father worries about you. He wants you to have a horse you can depend on.''

She shook her head, incredulous. ''You don't really believe that. You can't. This is hardly the first time I've taken a tumble since I climbed on a horse. Father isn't— He doesn't—'' Fury boiled up, and the sharp tang of grief, too new and raw for words. ''I messed up taking that drop jump. The fault was mine, not Dandy's. I told Father that, but he wouldn't listen. He never does.''

Maggie's nose was running again. She sniffed as she turned to open her closet. She wanted her riding boots. What she would do with them when she no longer had a horse she wasn't sure, but she refused to leave them behind. When she came out of the closet, boots dangling awkwardly from her left hand, her mother was gone. No surprise there. Sharon shied from confrontations the way a timid mare started at every scrap of litter tumbled by the wind.

Like mother, like daughter. Maggie grimaced and looked around for her purse.

It was gone, too.

Her first reaction was disbelief. It had to be here. She'd just jammed her address book in it. Yet the only possible reason for its disappearance was so absurd she put down her boots and hunted anyway.

Not that there were many places to look. Maggie carried her clutter with her in a satchel-size handbag, and kept her living space ruthlessly neat. She checked the closet, then crouched to look under the bed. And all the while her heart was hammering, hammering. Because she knew. Even though she looked, she knew she wouldn't find her purse.

Her mother had taken it.

Maggie sat back on her heels, sniffing furiously. It was such a silly, useless betrayal. Did her mother really think she could keep Maggie from leaving this way? But when had Sharon Stewart been anything but ineffectual? Sweet and gentle…and weak. Especially when it came to standing up to her husband on her daughter's behalf.

She needed her purse. It held her car keys, ID, credit cards, cash—all necessary, but all replaceable. More important were the things she couldn't replace. A favorite necklace with a broken catch she'd been meaning to have fixed. The plastic keys her friends' babies liked to play with and the Swiss army knife her brother had given her when she was eighteen. Photographs. Her high school ring, her address book and her favorite pen and…her journal.

Oh Lord. Her journal was in her purse.

The thought pushed Maggie to her feet. *Not this time,* she thought. This time she wasn't letting her mother off the hook. Sharon could stand by her man all she wanted.

This time Maggie wasn't going to pretend it meant anything less than betraying her daughter.

She shrugged into the only coat that fit over her cast, the scruffy leather bomber jacket she'd bought in the men's department years ago. Her mother hated it. Then she grabbed the strap on her wheeled suitcase and dragged it after her.

The broad, shallow stairs that swept from the second floor to the first would have done credit to Tara. Oil paintings in gilded frames kept pace with the broad, shallow steps, paintings hung on creamy walls that had never known the indignity of a fingerprint. Maggie paid no attention to them, or to the way her wrist throbbed as she and her suitcase thumped down those broad stairs. A fine, high tide of anger carried her along.

Halfway down, she heard her mother talking to someone in the foyer. All she could see of the visitor was a pair of cowboy boots.

It wouldn't be a salesman. Salesmen, strangers and missionaries on bicycles never came to this house. Importunities were delivered here more graciously, and on a grander scale. A congressman might hint at the need for donations to his campaign after dinner. The wife of a CEO might let it be known over cocktails that she was raising funds for her favorite charity. It was a house for soft voices, afternoon teas and elegant parties where lives and hearts could be broken with quiet, deadly courtesy.

Maggie paused. No problem, she decided. For once, she was ready to ride the angry tide into unfamiliar territory. So what if there was a scene? A rude, crashing, public scene might be just what she needed.

She raised her voice as she started the suitcase moving again. ''Don't you think I'm a little too old to be grounded, Mom?''

"Margaret, please." Sharon's voice was strained. "We'll discuss this later."

"Later doesn't work for me." Her riding boots felt as if they weighed thirty pounds apiece, and her wrist had gone from throbbing to a hard, solid ache and her suitcase kept trying to topple over. She didn't care. "I want my purse back. Now."

"We have company."

"Fine. Maybe he can tell me what you did with my purse. Or did you hide it before you answered the door?"

As her suitcase bumped along behind her, she saw more of the visitor—long legs encased in jeans that had faded to white in all those interesting places a man's body shapes wear into denim.

Maggie's heart did a quick, funny flip as something less distinct than memory, more painful than instinct kicked in. Her attention split between wrestling her suitcase down the stairs and the man who was revealed, step by bumpy step. She couldn't see his face because he stood on the other side of her mother, but she saw enough—a strong thigh and slim hip covered in worn denim. Part of a chest, a shoulder and arm wearing red cotton. At least, the shirt had once been red. Now it was worn and soft, the color faded to a deep rose.

And she saw his hand. Long-fingered and incongruously elegant, that hand. It held a dark brown Stetson...and it was dusted by dark hair on the back, though she couldn't see that from here. No more than she could see the thin white scar on the palm.

Memory supplied those details.

Maggie stopped dead. Her suitcase jerked on its strap, then toppled onto its side. She didn't notice. The breath caught in her throat and tangled there with the quick pumping of her heart.

''I seem to have come at a bad time,'' the visitor said, and stepped out from behind her mother.

It was a good thing she'd stopped moving. Otherwise she might have pitched forward physically when she fell into the bright dazzle of Luke's smile.

Lucas West was a sight to bedazzle any woman. His hair was a warm brown that always looked a few weeks late for a trim, just shaggy enough to invite feminine fingers. His skin was tanned, roughened by wind and sun, and his body was lean, strong-shouldered, with a cowboy's narrow hips and small, tight butt. The features on his narrow face were sculpture-perfect, right down to the most kissable mouth on either side of the Red River. But it was those eyes—those bright-as-sin, fallen angel eyes—that truly trapped a woman.

Oh, yes. Luke was appallingly good-looking. And he knew it.

Maggie scowled and bent to shove her suitcase upright and get her breathing started again. ''Your timing's not bad,'' she said, straightening. ''I was just about to leave, but I can't go until my mother gives me back my purse. She's trying to keep me from running away from home. What's new with you?''

''Not much. I sold Hunter's Child last week, and I expect I'll have a sister-in-law or two soon. But you already know about that situation.'' Smile lines traced friendly paths around eyes as wild as the bluebonnets that flooded hillsides in the spring. Deeper grooves cut his cheeks like parentheses, enclosing that sinful grin. ''Jacob would have explained when he proposed to you.''

Sharon gasped. ''Jacob West asked you to marry him? Margaret, you didn't tell me. You know your father was hoping—and Jacob is a wonderful man, so clever.''

''So rich, you mean. I turned him down.''

"That's what I heard." Luke's voice was mild, but some dark, unlikely emotion flashed through those bright eyes, gone too quickly to disturb the lazy grin. "That's why I'm here. That...and Fine Dandy."

"Dandy's gone." Grief pinched, too raw and private for words. She scowled at her mother, and the giddy zing of anger returned. "So is my purse."

Sharon's cheeks turned pink. "It's hardly my fault if you misplace your things."

Maggie thudded down the last two steps. "I didn't misplace it. You did. On purpose. Where is it?"

"Since you *insist* on discussing this now..." Sharon's lips tightened. "I locked it in the Cadillac."

Maggie's confidence stumbled. "I could break a window."

Sharon didn't bother to respond. They both knew she wouldn't. Not on her father's car.

"Maybe I can help." Luke moved closer.

"Please don't," Sharon said. "This is a family matter."

Maggie's eyebrows lifted. "You know how to break into a car?"

"I probably could," he admitted. "But I had a different sort of assistance in mind. I saw Fine Dandy listed when I was checking out some Web sites, looked into it and learned that your father had put him up for sale. So I bought him."

Hurt bit, mixing with anger and the lingering punch of arousal. "Great. That's wonderful. I'm very happy for you. Now get the heck out of—"

"Maggie!" her mother exclaimed, shocked.

"No, it's okay." Luke's eyes didn't leave her face. "I thought we might be able to work out a deal."

Her eyes narrowed suspiciously. "What kind of deal?"

"Marry me and you can have your horse back, enough money to continue competing—and me for a trainer."

She didn't even blink. "Why not? I've got nothing better to do."

Two

The front door closed behind Lacy Gray. Maggie was sure that the other woman so on so on, but she didn't not saddling the horse herself.

Two

The front door closed behind Luke firmly. Maggie had allowed him to take her suitcase and boots, but she clutched her saddlebag-size purse herself.

"My mother is not happy with you," she said cheerfully. "She wasn't crazy about it when you offered to spring me. Then you threatened my father's car. Serious penalty points there, Luke."

Luke glanced at the woman who was all but skipping along beside him on the way to his pickup. Maggie wasn't much bigger than a bite, but her pint-size body held enough energy for any three normal people. Her cheeks were round and freckled, her hair was very short, but otherwise undecided—neither curly nor straight, brown nor blond. Her clothes were more definite, being divided between the defiant and the sloppy. Above wrinkled khaki pants, her T-shirt was a scream of purple. The brown leather bomber jacket she wore looked like it had been through at least one World War. The cast that peeked out of her left sleeve was a radioactive-green.

And she had a small, husky voice. A whiskey-and-sin voice that made a man think of rumpled sheets. He wanted to jump her bones. "I like your shirt."

She glanced down at her chest. Yellow letters sprawled across the modest bumps made by her breasts asked, What Would Xena Do? She grinned. "It's a reminder. Part of my antiwuss campaign."

"Wuss?" His eyebrows lifted. "I've seen you compete. You could give lessons in determination to the Cowboys' offensive line. Maybe you should, after their last season."

"Oh, I'm fine on the back of a horse. It isn't until I'm standing on my own two feet that my wuss tendencies take over. If you hadn't forced things, I probably would have wimped out and left without my purse."

He paused, his head cocked to one side, trying to figure out what was going on. He'd expected to have a hell of a lot more trouble talking her into this, but she was grinning at him as if they ran off together every other week. "You're enjoying yourself, aren't you?"

"Damned right I am." She said it with a certain relish.

"That's three." He opened the pickup's passenger door.

"What?"

"That's the third time I can remember hearing you use a cuss word."

"The habits of a lifetime are hard to break. I'm working on it."

"Learning to cuss is part of your antiwuss campaign?"

"Yep." She tossed her purse onto the seat and climbed in. "Would you really have busted a window on my father's car if my mother hadn't given in and unlocked it?"

He grinned. "Damned right I would." Sitting on the bench seat of the pickup cab, she was slightly above him. He liked the perspective that gave him on those soft, smiling lips. He wasn't crazy about the rush of heat and frustration that hit, along with the tantalizingly faint wash of memories.

He'd have to get used to that. "We couldn't leave without your purse. You'll need ID when we get to Vegas."

"Oh, right. Of course. My mother would have thought of that sooner or later, wouldn't she? If not, my father certainly would have when he got back. Then they'd never have believed we were really running away to get married."

"Ah." He nodded. "Now I understand. You don't think this elopement is for real. You just want your father to think it is."

"Well...the fact that he can't stand you is a real plus, I'll admit. I haven't thanked you, Luke, but I do appreciate it. Asking me to run off with you was inspired. You think fast on your feet." She chuckled. "The look on my mother's face...anyway, I guess you came by to offer me a chance to ride Fine Dandy for you once my wrist is better, and I really, really appreciate that."

"I do want you to ride Fine Dandy."

"Then I'm sure we can work something out." In the same friendly tone she added, "But I do wish you'd stop staring at my mouth that way."

"I've always been partial to your mouth."

"No offense, but you're partial to any pair of lips attached to a female body."

The sudden grinding in his gut—was it anger? Or guilt? "Only the pretty ones." He tossed her suitcase in the back of the truck and climbed in on his side. "We'd better get going. The flight leaves at one-twenty."

"You have a flight to catch? I guess you could drop me at Linda's—her place is on the way. Or I can call someone from the airport to come get me. But maybe we could talk about Fine Dandy first?"

"No, Maggie, I don't have a flight to catch. *We* do. For Las Vegas."

Her eyes went huge, and her mouth parted—but no words came out. Satisfied, he started the engine.

The driveway was a long, concrete yawn leading to an equally boring street. Expensive—but boring. The houses here had grounds, not yards, and they were cared for by professionals. A three-man crew was stringing Christmas lights in the naked branches of several live oaks at one home.

Automatically Luke's gaze flickered and veered away.

He hated winter, hated the empty trees and sky, the creeping gray defeat of the season. Christmas was a hurdle to be leaped, the red-and-green mania that swept the world every December a trial to be endured before he could settle in to wait for the promise of spring.

"Okay, Luke," Maggie said abruptly. "It was a good joke. But enough is enough. You don't want to marry me."

"I don't?"

"I suppose I'm not the *last* woman you'd want to marry, but there must be a hundred or two you'd prefer. They can't have all turned you down already."

"I haven't asked anyone else."

Silence. They pulled to a stop at the light and waited for the light to change, and she didn't say a word—but he could almost hear her scrambling to pull her scattered thoughts together. He decided to help her out. "You know why I have to marry someone, the quicker the better, don't you? Jacob must have told you about Ada when he proposed.''

''Well—well, yes, he did.'' She shook her head. ''This is so weird. In twenty-seven years I've collected exactly zero proposals of marriage, then last week Jacob...and now you...and neither one of you—you're both *friends!*'' Her breath huffed out. ''This is just so weird.''

That was one word for it. Luke did take some satisfaction from hearing that Maggie thought of Jacob as a friend. ''This proposing business comes as a shock to me, too.''

Two weeks ago, if anyone had suggested to Luke that he would ever dabble in matrimony, he would have laughed. But two weeks ago, he hadn't known about Ada.

People outside the family didn't understand. To them, Ada was just a servant—first his father's housekeeper, now Jacob's. But to the West brothers, she was much more. She was the one woman they all loved, the one constant in their lives. No matter who else had come and gone—and there had been one hell of a lot of comings and goings—Ada had always been there for them.

And now she was dying. Or she would be, if she didn't continue the experimental treatments Jacob had arranged—the incredibly expensive, near-miraculous treatments at a Swiss research center. The only way to save her was for the brothers to do what they'd each sworn never to do.

They each had to marry. And fast.

Luke had turned onto the ramp to the Interstate before Maggie spoke again. ''Jacob did tell me about Ada's illness. And I honor you and your brothers for wanting to take care of her. That's wonderful. But I don't understand why—''

"You know the way my father left his estate tied up." He stamped on the gas harder than necessary. His father might be five years' dead, but he still had the power to make Luke want to be somewhere, anywhere, other than where he was. "Everyone does. I've seen articles about the trust in the *New York Times,* for God's sake."

"Yes, I know about the trust. Your father had some very peculiar views about marriage, Luke."

His grin flickered to life. "Tell me about it." After seven marriages to six women—he'd married and divorced Luke's mother twice—any other man might have been a little sour on the institution. Not Randolph West. He'd been enthusiastically planning his eighth wedding when a heart attack had ended his participation in the matrimonial sweepstakes.

"What I don't understand is why *you* have to get married."

"I hadn't planned on it." But life was forcing some changes in his plans. He'd sure as hell never intended to marry. He didn't need his inheritance, didn't want it. The ranch was *his.* He'd worked hard to build it and his reputation as a rider and a trainer. What he needed a lot more than money was a good rider, someone to handle some of the competitions where the horses gained both experience and the attention of potential buyers. He was getting stretched pretty thin.

He glanced at the woman beside him. Maggie was a damned fine rider. Maybe after their marriage ended…no, he thought, shaking off the thought. He was going to do his damnedest to make sure they came out of this friends. That was enough to hope for. "Even Jacob can't pay for Ada's treatments by himself," he said.

"I know that. But…Luke, I know you don't like talking about it, but you were married at one time. Doesn't that fulfill the conditions of the will as far as you're concerned? Or is there some stipulation about how long the marriage has to last?''

His fingers tightened on the steering wheel. ''No.'' Meaning *no* to both questions, *no* to the memories. *No* to the whole, sorry subject.

She didn't say anything, but she watched him expectantly, her hazel eyes solemn.

Dammit. This was the reason—one of the reasons— he'd always kept things light with Maggie. Casual friends, some teasing, a little flirting. No touching, no dating, no real come-ons. Not many people even knew about Pam, but Maggie did. She was Pam's cousin. They'd roomed together in college. She'd been at the hospital that night...

Only he hadn't always kept things light, had he?

''My father might have been slightly nuts on the subject of marriage,'' he said, ''but he wasn't a hypocrite. His will doesn't stipulate how long our marriages have to last, but all three of us have to be married when we petition to have the trust dissolved and stay married until it is. Pam and I divorced nearly ten years ago. Our brief, unlamented union doesn't count.''

''Oh.'' The hand without the cast started pleating the fabric of her T-shirt. ''I see why you have to marry, then. But...I'm sorry, but that isn't a reason for *me* to get married. There must be a thousand women right here in Dallas who would gladly take you on. And if we include the rest of Texas, why, the number would get sky-high.'' She smiled at him hopefully.

''Thanks,'' he said dryly. ''But there certainly aren't a thousand women I'm willing to marry.''

''But why *me?*''

He glanced at her, surprised. ''Because I know you. If

we agree on terms, I won't have to worry about you deciding you want more and stirring up trouble trying to get it. This marriage..." He laughed, short and hard. "God, my throat tries to close up when I say the word. You know that about me, know that there's no point in expecting too much, and there's another reason to ask you. I can't think of much worse than to be legally tied to a woman who thinks she's in love with me."

"Your ego's showing."

He shrugged. He knew himself. And he knew women. "With you...we can make things come out even, you and me. I need to get the trust dissolved. You need Dandy. Besides..." He grinned. "I like you."

"Luke." She sighed. "I like you, too. That's part of the problem. We're friends. I don't want to mess with that."

"We already did." He didn't look at her. "About a week before Christmas last year, we messed things up pretty thoroughly."

"Oh, that!" Her breezy voice dismissed it. "That was a mistake, of course. A mutual mistake. We were both a little tipsy, a little emotional. But we're adults, so we admitted we'd been a pair of prize idiots and put it behind us."

No, he thought. They hadn't put it behind them. They'd pretended it never happened. That was how she'd wanted to play it—how she still wanted to play it, obviously, and if he had some ideas about changing that, they could wait. "You're right," he said mildly. "We're friends. I don't want to lose that."

"Okay, then." She beamed at him like a teacher whose slowest student has finally given the correct answer. "We don't want to risk our friendship on something as—as uncertain as marriage. Even a businesslike marriage can get sticky.''

She said the right things, said them with such matter-of-fact good humor that he might have believed her...if her hands hadn't stretched the hem of her T-shirt all out of shape with their nervous pleating and unpleating. Or if he hadn't remembered all too well the look in her eyes when he'd climbed out of her bed, given her a kiss and walked out the door.

She would probably try to climb out of the truck right here on the Interstate if he let on that he knew he'd hurt her. ''I can't argue with you about marriage being an uncertain business.''

''Exactly.''

''But it's uncertain because people go into it with a lot of unrealistic expectations. We'll make sure we're both clear on what we want and expect from our deal. No emotions, no complications.''

''Luke...I'm sorry, but I don't *want* to marry you.''

''But you do want Fine Dandy. And you want to continue to compete. I know you'd rather have a marriage based on the good stuff,'' he said gently. ''You deserve it—flowers and pretty words, moonlight and promises. Romance.''

''Romance? Good grief. You know me. Practical as a pair of old boots.''

He had his work cut out for him, all right. ''Well, this would be a very practical way to meet both our needs.'' *Needs* might have been the wrong word to use. It conjured vague, heated memories he couldn't afford to indulge. ''Think of it as a business arrangement.''

The stubby arcs of her eyelashes blinked once, slowly. ''Like a marriage of convenience?''

''I guess.'' He hadn't heard the term before, and

wasn't sure what she meant. "If it were anyone else, I'd have to get a prenuptial agreement first. But I trust you. If we can agree to terms, I know you'll honor them."

She was thoughtful now, her fingers rubbing at her cast as if the wrist beneath it ached. "The problem is, I don't trust you."

"Ouch. I guess we can set our agreement down in writing. I'm thinking a million would be about right, once the trust has been dissolved."

"I don't—it isn't—good grief, a million dollars? You can't seriously propose to give me that kind of money!"

"Sure I can. I don't know exactly what my share of the trust will come to, but a million won't make that much of a dent in it."

"You know what? You're going to be a very rich man, Luke. I think you'll need a bodyguard more than a wife to protect you from all the women who will be scaling fences and swimming rivers to get to you." She chuckled.

Damn, he wished she wouldn't do that. Her voice was whiskey and sex; her chuckle was worse. "A bodyguard would cramp my style."

"And a wife wouldn't?"

Best not to touch that. "So, do you want to run by the lawyer's office and see how fast he can draw up some kind of prenuptial agreement?"

"I trust you about the money." Her hands started fiddling again, this time with the zipper on her jacket. Up, down. Up, down.

"If you trust me about the money, then where's the problem?"

"Sex."

The truck swerved slightly in the lane.

"How long will this marriage have to last to get the

trust dissolved once you're all married? Two months? Six?''

''Maybe four months.'' He had control of the truck, and himself, again. ''Maybe more. I'm not the financial whiz in the family, but Jacob's best guess is between four and eight months.''

''Well, I'm not crazy about getting a lot of pitying looks for the next four months or more because my husband has been seeing other women.''

His jaw tightened. ''You think I'd embarrass you that way?''

She shrugged and went back to toying with the zipper. ''I think you'd try to be discreet. The thing is, I *do* know you, Luke. Are you planning to swear off sex for the next four to eight months?''

He shot her an incredulous look.

She grinned. ''For once, I can read your mind.''

No, she couldn't. Or she'd be trying to climb out of the truck right now. Fortunately she hadn't a clue what kind of images had popped into his head when she'd said ''sex.''

But she'd been on target with the rest of it. Not that he'd actually thought it out. About all he'd taken the time to plan was how to get the two of them to Vegas as quickly as possible. But in the back of his mind, he'd assumed he'd find what he needed elsewhere...because no way was he going to hurt Maggie again. And sure as God made little green apples, if he took her to bed, she'd end up hurting.

But he hadn't thought it through. Maggie talked tough. She *was* tough, strong as old leather—in some ways. In others, she was as soft and easily damaged as a rose petal. Fragile. If he married her and then fooled around on her—never mind the reason for the marriage—he'd bruise that petal. Again.

Guilt rose, thick and grim. "I think they include something about fidelity in the marriage vows, even in Las Vegas. You don't think you could trust me to live up to any promises I make?"

"Luke." Her sigh was small, husky, impatient. "They include something about 'till death do us part' in those vows, too. But we wouldn't either one of us mean that part, would we?"

He couldn't think of a damned thing to say.

"I take it this means that the marriage is off." She shook her head. "Do you think we set any records for the shortest engagement ever? We're nearly to the airport, I see. I can call someone from there to come get me."

The hell of it was, he knew he could change her mind. Maggie wanted him. She didn't like it, tried to hide it, but the simmer and spark were there between them. Always had been. If he could get his hands on her, he could persuade her to marry him...among other things.

Hell, she was right not to trust him. Just as well he had to keep his hands on the wheel—it forced him to do this right. Changing her mind while threading his way through the seventy-mile-an-hour traffic on I-35 was going to be tricky, though. "Let me see if I understand. You won't marry me because you think I wouldn't be faithful."

"That's about it."

"Thought you'd found a deal-breaker, didn't you?" He grinned. "All right. I promise I won't fool around."

"I—I didn't exactly say I would marry you, even if— and realistically, a promise like that...Luke, have you

ever been faithful to any woman for longer than, say, a
week?''

"Realistically," he said gently, "I don't break promises. And this one is from me to you. Personal, not part
of whatever vows we make in order to dissolve the
trust." His quick glance revealed that she'd gone from
messing with the zipper to gnawing on her lip. "You're
cute when you're worried."

"I'm not worried."

"You're cute when you lie, too."

"And I'm not marrying you."

"Do you want me to promise that I won't use you,
Maggie? That I won't take you to bed just because you're
handy and I'm horny?"

Her cheeks flamed. "That sounds awful."

"It's what you're worried about, isn't it? All right.
You have my promise. I won't cheat on you, and I won't
use you." It wasn't a hard promise to give. Keeping
it...well, he'd have to, that was all.

She was staring unhappily at her lap, where the fingers
of her right hand were rubbing at the hand that was par-
tially encased in that radioactive-green cast. "You're not
used to celibacy, Luke."

"No." Time to lighten the mood, he decided, and
flashed her a quick grin. "I won't ask for a reciprocal
promise, however. Feel free to use me. If, at any time,
you become overwhelmed with lust—"

"Hah!"

"—my body is at your disposal."

She muttered something under her breath, scowling at
her clenched hands.

"I didn't catch that."

"Nothing. This just isn't a good idea, Luke."

"What's wrong with it? You get Fine Dandy, I get

what I need to take care of Ada and your father will be mad enough to spit nails." Malcolm Stewart couldn't stand him. He blamed Luke for everything that had gone wrong in that short, miserable marriage so many years ago.

With some reason, Luke knew.

"Now, there's a great reason to get married," she said dryly. "To irritate my father." But at last her hands stopped tormenting her T-shirt.

"Think of it as a bonus." This time, he'd be careful with her. He'd find a way to make her feel better about herself, to repair some of the damage he'd done. This time, he wouldn't hurt her when he left. "Here's another bonus. You need a trainer."

"Yes, but—but do you mean you'd do it? You'd be my trainer?"

"Yes."

"You're good." That was said grudgingly. "Almost as good as you think you are."

He grinned and signaled for the turnoff to the airport. "Better than Walt Hitchcock, anyway." He glanced at her. "Come on, Maggie. What would Xena do?"

She looked all over the place—at her shirt, her hands, out the window—everywhere but at him. And at last said, "Well…well, *hell*. I guess I will marry you, Luke."

6:54 p.m.

Five hours later, they stood side by side in the "Love Me Tender" wedding chapel just off the Strip. Candles burned atop the unused piano. A few minutes ago, a stereo had played the chapel's theme song while Maggie walked down a short aisle between empty pews.

The room was silent now, except for the words being spoken by the man in front of them.

Her mouth was dry. Her stomach was in revolt. In one hand she held a small bouquet of roses, while the other was clasped firmly in Luke's. His palm was dry, unlike hers. The scent of the roses blended unhappily with the floral room freshener someone had recently sprayed in the small room.

She was still wearing her purple T-shirt and cargo pants.

The man who was marrying them wore a collarless black shirt that looked vaguely ecclesiastical. His thin black hair was combed back meticulously over the bald spot on top of his head. His tanned skin was stretched so tightly over his cheeks that she was afraid it would split if he smiled.

Face-lift, she thought vaguely. She wondered if it hurt when he went to the dentist and had to "open wide."

Did ministers get face-lifts? *Was* he a minister? Panic clutched the pit of her stomach. She couldn't remember. She remembered picking out the music and the flowers, and discussing what version of the marriage ceremony they wanted. Why couldn't she remember who was marrying them? It seemed suddenly, vitally important to know. Was she making vows she didn't intend to keep before a man of God or a civil servant?

He'd stopped talking and was looking at her expectantly. Luke squeezed her hand.

She blinked. "Oh, ah—I do." What had she just promised?

She was losing it. She was truly losing it. What kind of woman didn't even hear the words of her wedding service?

A terrified woman.

Maggie made herself listen carefully as the man who might or might not be a minister went through his spiel again with Luke. It sounded pretty standard...and awfully final.

Luke's voice came out clear and strong. "I do."

Then there were the rings, one for each of them, and more words to repeat. The double-ring ceremony had been Luke's idea. She'd teased him about trying to buy a 24-carat bodyguard to protect him from all those man-and-money-hungry women who would soon be after him. She'd pointed out that even after they divorced, he could wear the ring sometimes to deter predators.

That had to have been one of the best performances of her life.

Her hand was shaking when she held it out so he could slip one of those rings on her finger. It stuck at the knuckle. "Uh-oh. My fingers are swollen from the cast."

"No problem." He grabbed her right hand. "You can switch it later."

So he slid her ring onto the wrong finger. *It doesn't mean anything,* she told herself. The ring meant nothing, just as the wedding meant nothing. And she was not going to throw up. She was definitely not going to throw up.

His ring, at least, fit perfectly.

The minister—if that's what he was—managed to smile without splitting his skin. "You may kiss the bride."

Luke's hands moved to her shoulders, and he turned her to face him. There was a smile on his lips, but his eyes looked old and sad. Apparently this mockery of marriage didn't scare him the way it did her. It just made him miserable.

He bent and brushed his lips across hers. "Buck up," he whispered. "The worst is over."

Her mouth tingled and her skin flushed from the brief touch of his mouth. Oh, help. What had she done?

This time would be different, she told herself firmly. This time she had nothing to prove—though she did have an agenda, one she hadn't told him about. One she prayed she'd have the courage to act on.

And this time, she knew beyond a shadow of a doubt that she wasn't in love with him.

Three

11:58 p.m.

Five hours and several hundred miles later, Maggie was feeling a lot better.

The stars were blisteringly bright this far from the city, and the darkness was huge. It was cut by the twin beams of the truck's headlights, interrupted here and there by distant dots of light from scattered houses. Inside the truck it was dark, too, save for the glow of the dashlights. And quiet, save for the low, bluesy throb of the music from one of Luke's CDs. Luke liked country and western music for dancing, she knew, but preferred jazz or blues for listening.

He smelled good.

Maggie leaned her head against the window, her eyes closed, drowsily enjoying the music and the faint, familiar scent of the man she'd impulsively married. It was going to work. It was all going to work out just like she'd planned.

How silly she'd been to panic. On the plane ride back to Dallas turbulence had defeated her desire to escape in sleep. Instead she'd been forced to talk to Luke—and a good thing, too.

They'd talked about horses and horse people, riding and various events, and it had been blessedly normal. Like old times. She'd felt that flicker of connection again, just as she always did. Months could go by without her seeing Luke, but when they met again she'd feel that click of recognition, as if they hadn't truly been apart.

A friend like that was worth a lot. She yawned, comfortable with the night and the man. An easy quiet had fallen between them, the kind that old friends could enjoy. Yes, a friendship like this was more important than the distracting hum of desire.

An uneasy little frisson went through her. What did that say about her plan?

But their friendship had survived last year's mistake, she assured herself. And she'd learned her lesson. She'd keep her eyes open, her goals clear.

Feeling cramped and suddenly wide-awake, she straightened, stretching her legs.

"I thought you'd dozed off." Luke gave her a teasing grin. "Doesn't do much for a man's morale for his bride to fall asleep on him on their wedding night."

"You said that without even stuttering," she said admiringly. "Bride, I mean."

"I'm working on it. We're almost there," he added, slowing. The headlights flashed on the wintry skeletons of two enormous oaks as he turned onto the blacktop road they guarded.

"Good. It's been a long day, what with getting married and standing up to my father. In *absentia,* of course. I'm not quite up to doing that in person yet."

"We could have stayed in Vegas overnight."

He'd suggested that, offering to get a suite so they could have separate bedrooms. Maggie had vetoed the idea. Staying in a hotel with Luke had sounded entirely too intimate.

She really was an idiot, wasn't she? She was going to be living with the man, for heaven's sake. "This way I can see Dandy as soon as I get up in the morning."

"I imagine he'll be glad to see you." He glanced at her. "You've got one hell of a horse there, Maggie."

She beamed at him. "He is, isn't he?"

"I've seen the two of you compete. He's not a horse who worries about pleasing his rider, is he?"

"No, you have to prove yourself to him. He loves to compete. To win. That's why Walt told Father to get rid of him—he claims Dandy is too much horse for a *woman.*" She gave the last word an awful emphasis. "He said my fall proved he was right, that I couldn't control Dandy."

"All riders fall," he said mildly. "What happened, anyway?"

"It was my fault, but it didn't have anything to do with my gender. We were on a course I knew really well, just hitting it for practice, not speed, and I got sloppy. Didn't place him right before a jump, then overcompensated."

He nodded. "A familiar course can be more dangerous than a new one, because we stop paying attention." He yawned and ran a hand through his hair. "It's been a long day."

"Mmm-hmm." Luke had gorgeous hair. She'd always

liked the way it curled at his nape. It was longer than his brother's. Messier, too, which summed up a lot of the differences between him and Jacob. She liked his neck, too—it was strong and masculine, and the taste of his skin along the muscular cord that ran from jaw to collarbone, when he was slightly sweaty...

Down, girl. She shifted in her seat again.

"Maggie?" Luke's smile was quizzical. "You drifted off on me. If I didn't know better, I'd say you were nervous. You're not having wedding-night jitters, are you?"

Why did he keep referring to wedding nights? "Don't be silly. I've been traveling all day, I'm sleepy and I'm sick of sitting. And this isn't a real wedding night." No more than it had been a real wedding, even if the tight-skinned man who'd pronounced them man and wife *had* been a minister. Her ring wasn't on the right finger, and it was loose. She fiddled with it, turning it around and around. "I've never been to your ranch. It's funny to think I'll be living someplace I've never seen."

"The house isn't fancy, but it's comfortable. You'll like the stable."

He'd told her about his place on the plane—well, not about the house, but the important parts—the stable, the riding ring and the grounds. There was an area for dressage and a course that could be varied for fieldwork. And there were the horses, his horses, the ones he bred and the ones he trained. She was eager to see everything, but it would have to wait for morning. It was too late now.

Too late... "Hey, is that your place up ahead?" she said quickly. "I see lights."

"That's it. I wish you could see it in the summer. Winter doesn't do the place justice."

By summer, they might already be divorced. Maggie ignored the tight, funny feeling in her stomach. "You'll

have to ask me back to see it sometime, then,'' she said
lightly.

By the time they pulled up in front of a rambling
ranch-style house, there were other lights to hold back
the inky-darkness of the country. One glowed above the
door to the stable; another rested atop a pole at the entrance to the driveway. Light poured from windows at
the house, and Sarita had left the porch light on for him.

The welcoming lights, the familiarity, kindled a
warmth in Luke's chest. This was his. It was a good
feeling.

Maggie hopped down from the truck before he could
get her door, which didn't surprise him. He did manage
to snag her suitcase. The cast slowed her down.

''I can get it.''

''Enjoy my fling with chivalry while it lasts,'' he told
her, heading for the door. ''Tomorrow, when I put you
through your paces, you'll be cursing me.''

''Tough trainer, huh?''

''Merciless.'' He swung the door open. ''Come on in.''

She wandered down the short hall to the living room.

''Wow.'' She stood in the center of the long living
area, turning slowly. ''This is great. It isn't what I expected, though.''

''I only put mirrors on the ceiling in my bedroom.''

Her laugh was low and husky. It ran through him like
invisible fingers, making him itch. Making him want. He
set her suitcase down and watched as she wandered
around the room, investigating the entertainment unit,
running a hand along the back of one of the leather
couches. She paused at the mantel to study the gold
medal that rested on a special stand beneath a glass dome.

She had no business having a laugh like that, not when

she looked like a hundred pounds of girl-next-door. Though that, too, was deceptive. Maggie was an athlete. Her build might be small, but it was all muscle. He gave that build an appraising and appreciative eye. "You're what—five-two? Five-three?

"Five-two."

"How much do you weigh?"

"Luke." Her sideways glance might, in another woman, have seemed flirtatious. But Maggie didn't flirt. "Don't you know better than to ask a woman her weight?"

"I'm your trainer."

"Oh." She flushed. "Right. One-twenty."

"You don't look it."

"The freckles add ten pounds. I want one of those," she said, nodding at the medal.

"Give it time. You're not ready yet."

The slight lift of her chin turned her suddenly haughty. "Oh? Walt Hitchcock thinks I am."

"Yeah, but he's an idiot."

"If you don't think I'm any good, why did you—"

"You're damned good. I wouldn't take you on if you weren't. But you can be better."

She met his eyes levelly for a moment, then nodded. "I will be."

He smiled, liking her attitude. Maggie might have some problems with self-esteem, but when it came to riding, she knew her worth. "Come on," he said, lifting her suitcase and heading for the bedroom wing. "It's late. I'll show you to your room."

Hard to understand how a woman as sexy as Maggie could have such major doubts about her appeal. He wasn't sure if her father was to blame, with his constant carping, or if the problem had started with that jerk she'd dated last year. Luke would have liked to blame it all on the jerk. She'd been looking for a friendly shoulder the night the man broke up with her. Unfortunately for her, she'd run into Luke. He'd ended up giving her more than his shoulder.

Well, he couldn't change what he'd done, couldn't undo the hurt, but he could make it up to her in other ways. He could give her Fine Dandy and see that she had a shot at the gold, but that wasn't enough. A rider of Maggie's caliber would do well with a number of trainers.

"That thing has wheels on it, you know."

"Hmm?" No, what Maggie really needed was something he was particularly suited to give her. She needed to believe in herself as a woman.

"The suitcase," she said. "You don't have to play macho man and carry it. If you put it down and pull on the little strap, it rolls along nicely."

"Smart-ass." He stopped at the door to the largest guest bedroom. "You're supposed to admire my manly muscles."

She chuckled. "I just know how much you want to impress me with your manliness, too. You've already crushed one of my illusions, you know. I was expecting a lot of bachelor clutter, a little dust, but everything's spotless."

"Shame on you for stereotyping." He opened the door and flipped on the light. "Of course, if Sarita didn't put sheets on the bed for you, we're in trouble. I have no idea where they are."

"Sarita?"

"My housekeeper. You'll meet her in the morning." He put her suitcase down on the old-fashioned quilt that covered the bed. "I called her right after I made the plane reservations and told her to get a room ready for you. I think we can count on fresh sheets.'' He turned to face her.

Maggie had stopped a foot inside the room. Her expression was cheerful, her posture relaxed and she had a two-handed, white-knuckled grip on her purse as if it was struggling to escape. ''I guess you told her about us getting married and—and everything.''

''About getting married, anyway.'' He moved toward her. ''There won't be any 'everything,' but I didn't mention that.''

She flushed and, at last, moved farther into the room, circling him to put her purse on the bench at the end of the bed. She glanced around the room brightly, looking everywhere except at him. ''Oh, this is nice. Homey and soothing, with all the blues and browns.''

''I can see how soothing you find it,'' he said dryly. She was ready to jump out of her skin just from standing in a bedroom with him. ''You know, when you blush, your skin and your freckles blend together.''

She rolled her eyes. ''Thanks very much.''

''That was a compliment, Maggie. You look pretty when you blush.'' He moved closer, cupped her cheek in one hand and touched softness. *Gently,* he reminded himself. He didn't want to scare her. ''Makes a man want to find out if your skin is as warm as it looks.''

She jerked her head back. ''Luke. I don't know what you're trying to do, but—''

''I'll show you,'' he said amiably. And bent and kissed her.

The charge that jolted through him surprised him— surprised him so much he forgot to pull away after brushing her lips once. He had to go back for another, deeper taste.

A small fist hit him squarely in the chest. Hard.

"Hey!" He stepped back. "A simple no would have worked."

"You keep your hands to yourself!" Both her hands were knotted into fists, even the one on the casted arm.

He rubbed his chest, scowling. For a little thing, she packed quite a wallop…in more ways than one. "I didn't touch you. I kissed you. There's a difference."

"I know what you did." She made it sound as if he'd torn her clothes off. "I should have known when you kept mentioning wedding nights that you'd try something."

Anger bit. "If I'd been trying to seduce you, Maggie, you'd be on your back in that bed right now. It was an impulse, not an attack. You looked pretty, so I kissed you."

She glared at him. "You can't go around kissing everyone you think looks pretty! No, wait—I guess you can. You *do*. But you can't go around kissing *me* whenever the urge strikes."

It occurred to him belatedly that her reaction had been perfect. If he forgot himself again when he was making her feel wanted, she'd punch him. Even through the remarkable haze of lust she inspired, that would get his attention.

He grinned, pleased with her. "I'm weak, but I can learn. If you clobber me like that every time I give in to the urge, maybe it will go away." He turned. "Go ahead and sleep in, if you like—it'll be your last chance for a while. After tomorrow, you'll be up early, running laps."

"I hate laps."

She sounded sulky. It made her voice huskier than ever. His hand tightened on the doorknob as another wave of heat hit. "Tough," he said, and shut the door firmly behind him.

Tomorrow, he thought, heading back to the living room, he'd start working with Fine Dandy and Maggie. He was looking forward to it. Dressage first, he thought, turning off the light. Dressage was the foundation for all the rest, and shouldn't strain that broken wrist too badly.

Instead of going straight to his room, he paused to appreciate the way the huge, undraped window at the back of the house let the night in. Stars spilled over each other overhead, a vast nightly show he never grew tired of.

He ached. Still. In fact, he was log-hard and ready for something that wasn't going to happen...not for several months, most likely. He thought about a cold shower and shook his head ruefully. How long would this marriage last? Four months? Six? Taking a cold shower once or twice a day for the next six months did not appeal.

It looked as though he was going to become more closely acquainted with himself in the next few months than he had been since Serena Sayers took him around the world in the back seat of her daddy's Chevy. Lord, that had been a long time ago. A lot of years had passed. A lot of women, too. Some would say too many—Maggie would, and did. But Luke liked women. He liked the way they looked and moved and thought, their moods and quirks, the mystery of them. They were tough and fragile all at once, and never wholly predictable. He wouldn't apologize for having enjoyed the women he'd known. And there was only one he truly regretted.

Thirst hit, quick and hot. He looked at his empty hands, and could almost see one of them curled around a glass half-filled with amber liquid. All too easy to picture that, to imagine the sweet burn of Scotch sliding down his throat. His mouth tightened.

It was the thought of Pam that did it, he supposed. Only rarely did he drink, and even more rarely did he crave a drink. Odd that he had such a distrust of the stuff, when it had been Michael's mother, not his, who'd fought a losing battle with the bottle. But he didn't handle alcohol well, never had. Drink made a fool of him, and he seldom indulged in more than a casual beer or glass of wine…except when the memories rose and choked him. It didn't happen often these days. No more than once a year.

It had been on one of those nights, the ones when he felt too sorry for himself, with too much already lost, for it to matter if he lost some small piece of himself in the bottle, that he'd run into Maggie last year. And proved he was still more of a fool drunk than sober.

Luke sighed. Well, he'd do what he could to make amends. It was a relief, a big one, to know that Maggie would stop him if he lost sight of his little-used nobility and tried to take her further than he should.

Tomorrow, he thought, turning away from the window, he'd see about getting Fine Dandy's ownership transferred to Maggie. Hitchcock was an idiot to have advised Malcolm Stewart to sell the horse. Maggie's big gelding had the heart, the smarts and the strength for eventing. In the right hands, Dandy could be a champion.

Just like his owner. Luke smiled as he entered his bedroom.

Whether she knew it or not, Maggie's training had already started.

Maggie sat in the middle of the big bed, the covers pulled up to her waist, her journal propped against her lifted knees. She was wearing her usual winter sleep-wear—raggedy sweats. The pants had once been red; the top was violently orange. She was chewing on the end of her pen after recording the events of this extraordinary day.

All in all, she finished, *I think my plan has an excellent chance of success. If one simple kiss can make me feel…*

She lifted her head, staring into space. The feeling was easily summoned, though memory was a pale creature compared to the original experience. But she couldn't find words for it. Not a tingle, no, nor an electric jolt…warmth? Yes, but the sun was warm, and this hadn't felt all light and pleasant, like sunshine.

If the night could be said to glow, then it had bloomed in her when Luke kissed her. She nodded and resumed writing.

…a dark heat, then how much more can he make me feel, given a chance? Not love—she underlined that—*not anymore. That's gone, thank goodness. If I'd doubted that, his kiss proved it to me. I didn't fall into his arms this time.*

She frowned. No, she hadn't. She'd hit him.

Oh, well. She shrugged and finished. *I'll be happy to settle for lust. If any man can cure me of this dreadful habit I have of freezing up during lovemaking, it's Luke. And judging by his behavior, I shouldn't have to seduce him—which is just as well, since I haven't a clue how to go about that. Being female and standing still seems to be enough to get his engine revved.*

She chewed on the end of her pen. She really ought to be more positive. *I'm not bad-looking, after all,* she added. *I've got good legs, even if they are on the short side. That and proximity should do the trick. But I am going to have to get over wanting to knock him into the next county when he touches me.*

She closed her pen inside the journal, set it on the bedside table and turned out the lamp. Then turned it back on, picked up the little book and jotted a P.S.: *I'd better buy some new nightgowns. Even Luke might have trouble getting turned on by baggy sweats.*

Four

"Like that, don't you?" Maggie murmured, rubbing the spot along Dandy's jaw that made him look as if he wanted to purr. "This is more what I expected, you know. The stable, the grounds. The house, though..." She shook her head.

She was alone except for half a dozen horses. Outside, the wind was whipping around, making a show of ushering in winter. Inside, the air was animal-warm and smelled comfortably of hay and horses and the sweet, nutty scent of feed. Dandy's big box stall had already been mucked out, as had the other occupied stalls. Luke ran a classy operation—but that was no more than she'd expected.

No, the stable held no surprises for her. His house had, though. It was truly a home.

Take her bedroom. There was a kilim rug spread on the varnished wood floor, a starburst quilt on the bed, an old-fashioned pitcher and bowl with a chipped rim on the bedside table. Maggie had showered and dressed quickly when she woke up, pulling on riding pants and boots and an old red sweater. Her riding gloves had gone in the pockets of her leather jacket—and then she'd gone exploring.

Luke's house was like him—thoroughly charming, and thoroughly masculine. In the living room, a woven rug covered part of the shiny wooden floor. The ceiling was canted and beamed, and one wall—the one that backed onto the kitchen—had been stripped to expose the brick. The couch and one chair were leather; there was an oversize chair and ottoman upholstered in faded green, and a set of andirons shaped like dragons guarded the fireplace. Nothing quite matched, but it all worked together in a comfortable whole. The effect was rustic and inviting. Homelike.

Nothing looked like it ought to, she thought now, frowning. Luke's house wasn't all polished the way her parents' house was, as if a designer had lifted a page from a magazine and pasted a 3-D version in place. But neither did it have the slightly stark, stereo-and-sofa look of a single man's dwelling.

Probably one of his women had helped him decorate. Her lip curled contemptuously. Or several of them.

The housekeeper had caught her investigating. Sarita didn't fit Maggie's preconceptions, either. Housekeepers were supposed to be plump and motherly. Luke's housekeeper was in her early twenties, and if she was a bit plump, her padding was in all the right places. She had a yard of shiny black hair and dark, disapproving eyes—at least, they'd certainly seemed to disapprove of Maggie.

It's none of my business, Maggie told herself, if Luke had had the bad taste to get involved with his employee.

He'd promised Maggie fidelity, and she would hold him to that. For as long as the marriage lasted.

Dandy nudged her shoulder with his big head. "Did I stop rubbing? Yes, all right, you greedy thing. I'm back at it now."

"I thought you were going to sleep in."

She turned her head. The people-size door in the middle of the stable was open, letting in cold air, sunshine and Luke. Like her, he was dressed for riding, and what those form-fitting pants did for his legs and butt ought to be illegal.

Her stomach went tight with nerves. "I did sleep in. It must be nearly nine o'clock."

He chuckled as he joined her at Dandy's stall. "More like eight-thirty."

"Well, that's sleeping in for me." The nerves didn't surprise her. She'd expected to feel them when she saw him again this morning. Should she have expected this quick punch of delight, as well? "I've always been a morning person. It's one of the few traits my father approves of." She grinned. "Which is why I tried my darnedest to turn into a night owl while I was in college, but I was spectacularly unsuccessful at it. Even when I stayed up all night, I couldn't get the knack of sleeping till noon."

His smile treated her to a glimpse of the dimple in his left cheek. "You must not have pulled the right kind of all-nighter."

What was she supposed to say? That all-night sex binges had been more Pam's speed than hers? Maggie knew better than to mention her cousin. Luke would get all tight and sad around the eyes, and change the subject. And she wasn't ready to mention sex.

Fortunately Dandy chose that moment to interrupt with

another nudge. "Spoiled creature," she said, relieved to have an excuse to turn away from Luke. "By the way, why didn't you tell me your housekeeper doesn't speak English?"

"There's nothing wrong with Sarita's English."

"Well, all I heard from her was Spanish. When she saw me in the dining room she looked so suspicious—like I'd been about to slip the silver in my pocket, or something. I tried to tell her who I was, but I run out of Spanish after *Buenos Dias* and *Yo quiero Taco Villa*."

He laughed. She liked to watch Luke laugh. He put his head back, as if to open his throat better to let the laughter out. "Sarita's mad at me. She won't let on that she understands a word of English until she's finished punishing me."

"But why wouldn't she speak to me? I haven't done anything to make her mad. Unless you—I mean, if she…" Maggie decided to shut up before she wedged more than her big toe in her mouth.

"The answer to the question you haven't asked is no." Luke's eyes twinkled. "Sarita wouldn't have me on a bet. Besides, she's married to one of my grooms. Ed's as good with the horses as Sarita is with an oven."

"Oh." That did reassure her. Luke might have all the constancy of a tomcat, but he was honest in his own way. He didn't lie, and he never, ever messed around with married women. "So why is she mad?"

"She doesn't approve of married couples having separate bedrooms."

"Oh."

"She lectured me about it all through breakfast. In Spanish."

She barely kept herself from saying "oh" again. "I see." She did, too—more than she wanted to. Sooner or later, everyone who worked here at the ranch would know Luke wasn't sleeping with his wife. Word would spread. It always did. And no one who heard the gossip would believe Luke had a problem, not with his reputation. They'd think there was something wrong with her.

They'd be right.

"Want to move into my bedroom so my housekeeper won't be mad at me?"

Her laugh held equal parts relief and humor. This kind of teasing she knew how to handle. "I don't think so. Want to introduce me to some of Dandy's stablemates?"

"Sure. We'll start with the ladies." He took her hand and led her to the next occupied stall, where a palomino mare had her head over the rail, obviously expecting attention. "This is Gotcha Girl."

The moment Luke's hand had closed around hers, Maggie had stiffened. In anger? Because it felt so good? It took all her concentration to keep her voice normal. "Funny name."

"She's a funny lady." He let go of her hand, thank goodness, to give the mare a scratch behind her ear. "Ed suggested the name when she was born, and it fits. Her sense of humor leans toward the obvious. She likes to surprise you with a little nip, a tug on your hair, whatever might make you jump. If you do, she gives this little whinny—*gotcha*." He gave the mare a last, affectionate pat. "She's out of Desert Gold and George's Girl. Polite as a princess in the dressage arena, fast as blue blazes and she has the makings of a good jumper, though she's young yet. Two blue ribbons at Training Level trials. I'm going to take her to Preliminary next year."

He took her around the stable, introducing her to his horses. And he kept touching her. On the arm, when he led her from one stall to the next. On the shoulder, when two of his hands came in, and he introduced them.

The touches were oh, so casual—but they didn't feel casual to Maggie. She was excruciatingly aware each time his hand rested on her. Not that she was hit with some wild compulsion to toss him to the floor and have her way with him. No, she just felt…more. Her fingertips absorbed more detail about the coarse coat of the gelding she stroked. The air seemed to move more sweetly through her lungs, and the play of light and shadows grew sharper, more distinct.

And each and every time he put his hand on her, she wanted to knock it off. Definitely, she thought, she was going to have to work on her attitude if she was going to get anywhere with her plan.

"The tack room is this way," he said at last, taking her elbow.

"Wait a minute. You've missed a few introductions." Subtly—at least, she hoped it was subtly—she slipped out of his grasp, gesturing at the far end of the stable. "What about the ponies at the end, and that bay quarter horse? I didn't know you'd started working with ponies."

"I'm not," he said curtly.

"Are they yours, or are you boarding them?"

He jammed his hands into his pockets, looking oddly ill at ease. "They're for my students."

"Students? You?"

"If you don't think I'd make much of a teacher, you shouldn't have accepted me as your trainer." He turned away.

"Wait a minute." This time it was Maggie who reached out to him, grabbing his arm. "Of course you'd be a good teacher. But I'm having trouble picturing you teaching the neighbor's kids to keep their heels down. Besides, when would you have time?"

"I don't teach the neighbor's kids. There's a group in Dallas I work with. They bring some boys out twice a week."

Twice a week? That was a pretty big commitment of time. And the ponies were here apparently just for these lessons. "So what group is this? And how come you never mentioned it?"

He shrugged. "Why would I? Come on. We've wasted enough of the morning. It's time to get to work."

Curious, she followed him into the tack room. It was meticulously organized, and smelled pleasantly of leather. Saddles sat on their racks, and halters, leads and bridles hung from pegs along the walls. "Nice," she said, looking over the equipment. Some of the gear was obviously sized for children. "You've spent a pretty penny on the stuff for your kids."

"They're not my kids." He took a bridle down. "See if you can find a dressage saddle that will fit. A schooling helmet, too. I want you up on Gotcha Girl this morning. I've seen you on Dandy. I want to see you on a horse you aren't used to."

He didn't want to talk about his students, did he? Well, she'd let him push the subject aside—for now.

Maggie went to look over the dressage saddles, which were made deeper in the seat than a jumping saddle, with the low part of the saddle well forward to keep the rider sitting easily above her feet. "This one might do for me, if it fits Gotcha Girl." She reached for it.

"What do you think you're doing?" He pushed her hands away.

"Getting ready to tack up?" she suggested.

In cool, precise terms he told her what he thought about her intelligence, ending by suggesting that if she overtaxed her wrist and had to take painkillers, she wouldn't be of any use to him or her horse.

Indignantly she said, ''I didn't even bring the painkillers with me. I don't whine over a little ache.''

''No, you don't whine. But apparently you don't have the sense to avoid straining an unhealed break. If you aren't bright enough to take care of yourself properly, I'll make you keep the arm in a sling every second you aren't on horseback.''

Her eyebrows lifted. ''Aye, aye, sir.''

''I'll tack up for you this morning. After this, get one of the hands or Ed to do it.''

''All right, already. I keep forgetting about the cast, that's all. I'm not used to it.''

''It isn't the cast that's the problem,'' he said curtly. ''It's the broken bone the cast is protecting. Try to remember that.'' He handed her the bridle, lifted the saddle and selected a pad and breastplate.

Interesting, she thought as she followed him out of the tack room. She'd always known there was a ruthless streak beneath Luke's easygoing grin; you didn't win an Olympic Gold by charming it out of the judges. But watching the casually sexy man who'd been teasing and touching for the past hour turn into a no-nonsense trainer was rather startling.

The stable was busier now. The hands she'd met earlier were leading two of the horses out, and a short, muscular young man was headed for the tack room. ''Ed, this is Maggie,'' Luke said easily. ''We got married last night.''

The young man grinned. ''So I heard. Glad to meet you, ma'am.'' Sarita's husband had dark, serious eyes and weight-lifter thighs that strained the material of his jeans. He spoke with a thick Texas accent. ''That's quite a horse you have. Mostly Thoroughbred, isn't he?''

She smiled back, pleased as always by a compliment to Dandy. "Thoroughbred on his father's side, Thoroughbred-warmblood mix from his mother. Wait until you see him on a course. He flies."

"I'm looking forward to it."

Luke grinned. "You'll get to see him on some jumps this afternoon when I put him through his paces."

"Wait a minute," she said. "I'm here now. I'll work Dandy."

"You can walk him. You won't jump him. Not with a broken wrist."

"Good grief, Luke, I'm not talking about steeplechase. I can put him over a few low fences without hurting my wrist."

"No. You can't." He didn't bother to look at her, switching the subject to stable business, discussing a possible change in feeding requirements with Ed.

Maggie felt dangerously close to pouting. She'd missed her horse, dammit. But Dandy was Luke's horse now, though he had promised to get the papers switched to her name as soon as possible. More to the point, Luke was her trainer. She sighed and resigned herself to a quiet walk on Dandy's back later.

"It was good to meet you, Mrs. West," Ed said with a friendly nod.

She blinked, startled. "I—ah—yes. Good to meet you, too, Ed."

She stood there, bemused, as the young man moved on into the tack room. Not until Luke moved away did she shake off the mood, following him to Gotcha Girl's stall. "That felt strange. Being called Mrs. West, I mean."

"I noticed," he said dryly. "You looked like you'd taken a kick to the head. Technically you're Maggie West now, but it's up to you. Would you rather use your maiden name?''

''Maiden name. That sounds so—so—'' She shook her head and opened the stall.

''Virginal?'' Luke chuckled, setting the saddle across the lower half of the stall door so he could put the pad on the mare's back. ''Don't worry. I doubt people will jump to that conclusion if you decide not to use my name.''

Inspiration struck. ''But we're sleeping in separate bedrooms. If I use my maiden name—well, it doesn't look like we're really married. Could someone challenge the legality of the marriage? Cause problems with dissolving the trust?''

Luke frowned and lifted the saddle in place. ''I don't know. I don't see why anyone would want to, but I'll talk to Jacob. He knows that world better than I do.''

Maggie started to slip the bridle on, but the mare took exception to the cast. She held her arm out and let the horse investigate it. ''There might be people who like things the way they are. Whoever administers the trust probably makes a pretty penny off of it.''

He snorted. ''Rufus Albright was father's personal attorney. He's the chief trustee, a prig and a pain in the ass. He's also so honest that priests could confess to him instead of the other way around.''

''Oh.'' Gotcha Girl seemed to have accepted the strange, hard thing on Maggie's arm, so Maggie offered the bit. The horse took it like a lady. ''I've heard my father talk business too often not to absorb a few things about it, whether I wanted to or not. The trust holds a lot of stock in a couple of major corporations, doesn't it? When that stock is distributed between you and your brothers, that will affect the way it's voted. Someone might not like the change.''

''I'll talk to Jacob.'' Luke checked the fit of the saddle carefully before fastening the breastplate.

Maggie moved automatically to the other side so she could buckle it in place there. ''If Jacob thinks someone might question our marriage because we aren't, uh—because we have separate bedrooms...''

Luke grinned at her over Gotcha Girl's back. ''Don't worry. Even if he thinks there might be a problem, I'm not going to insist on claiming my marital rights. No one can prove we aren't tearing up the sheets just because we have separate bedrooms. If anyone is crude enough to ask why we don't sleep together, I'll tell them you snore.''

''Thanks a lot.''

''Of course, if you were a virgin, that might complicate things. But since that isn't the case—''

''No. No, that, uh, isn't a problem.'' Darn and blast. For a minute, she'd thought she'd found the perfect reason to go to bed with Luke without the need for a lot of messy explanations. She could have nobly agreed to do whatever was necessary to make the dissolution of the trust proceed smoothly.

That would have been too easy, she supposed gloomily.

''Hey.'' He was adjusting the stirrups, but paused to looked at her over his shoulder. ''Is something wrong?''

''Not a thing.'' She smiled brightly. ''I notice you use an egg-butt snaffle. Is Gotcha Girl busy-mouthed?''

He studied her, his eyes dark and grave, oddly compelling. As if he were asking a question, one she couldn't refuse or ignore. Her heartbeat stuttered. She wanted to look away. And couldn't.

"Yes," he said at last. "She's very supple in the mouth. I train her with a caveson, and switch to a sliding figure-eight for competition." Finally he released her from his gaze, running his hand under the girth, checking the tightness. "Let's head to the arena and see what you can do with her."

"Right." She led the mare out of the stall, glad to escape the odd power of his eyes.

Five

Luke stood in the center of the arena, turning to keep track of the woman and the horse as they cantered slowly around. He watched her with a trainer's eyes, and with a man's. Both sides of him took pleasure in the sight. Watching Maggie Stewart ride was like watching music in motion.

Or Maggie West. She hadn't said which name she was going to use, had she?

"Okay, bring her down to a trot and come here," he said. The cast was giving her some trouble, he noted. She was too conscious of it. "Quit protecting your arm. It's making you stiff, which makes the jarring worse. Loosen up. Follow the motion from the hips, not the shoulders."

She gave a businesslike nod.

"She's had enough fun. Time to make her work. Start with some circles and watch her shoulders. She's got a tendency to pop her inside shoulder." The trainer contin-

ued to watch, to note problems, strengths, the fluidity of
her spine and the perfect three-point seat. The man noticed other things.

Her riding pants fit like a second skin. That's how they
were supposed to fit, of course—snugly enough that no
fold of cloth could rub or chafe. But Luke appreciated
that fit with more than professional interest. Maggie's
rear was firm and round and deliciously female. Her
calves disappeared into the tall riding boots, but her
thighs were lovingly revealed.

He wanted his hands on those thighs, or cupping that
curvy bottom. He'd had thoughts, urges, like that around
Maggie before, especially since leaving her bed last
Christmas—even though he couldn't remember what had
happened in that bed. But the thoughts were more intru-
sive now. Stronger. It was hard to keep his mind on one
kind of form, and off the other.

"Counter-canter," he called, and watched as she ap-
plied the aids that cued the horse into a flying lead change
and a smooth, flowing turn. Beautiful. Only those intimately familiar with the subtle signals used in dressage
would have seen the tiny shifts of legs and seat that told
the horse what to do. Woman and horse moved together
as if guided by a single thought.

It was only natural that desire would bite harder now,
he supposed. She was living with him. Technically she
was his wife. Just as technically she was Maggie West
now. And there was no reason for his ego to get in a
twist over whether or not she used his name. This was a
business deal, not a real marriage.

Not that he had any clue what a real marriage involved,
except for sex. Luke understood sex, the closeness and
warmth as well as the sheer physical splendor of the act.

But a real marriage had to involve more than sweaty bodies, didn't it? Things like trust, friendship, fidelity.

Two out of three, he thought. He could bring two out of three of those qualities to a marriage. But trust and friendship weren't enough, even with great sex added. Fidelity—real fidelity—didn't come with a time limit. How long would he have to keep his promise to Maggie—six months? More? He would do it. For however long their marriage lasted, he would be faithful, but celibacy was already wearing thin.

And that, he supposed, was the main difference between his arrangement with Maggie and a real marriage. The real thing didn't come with an expiration date.

He wondered as he called out directions if he'd ever seen a real marriage.

Most marriages were no more than legalized affairs, from what he could see. Friendship, that's what mattered. Loyalty. Fidelity might be foreign to Luke, but he understood loyalty. Which was why he wasn't about to let the most mindless part of his body determine how he handled things with Maggie. He intended to make sure they were still friends when this arrangement of theirs ended.

But it sure felt strange to have her living in his house.

"Okay, that's enough for today," he said, moving closer as she and Gotcha Girl came to a stop. "How's the wrist?"

"Throbbing," she admitted. "Much as it grieves me to admit it, you were right. I can't jump Dandy yet."

"Amazing. You practically admitted you were wrong."

"And that," she said severely, "comes perilously close to 'I told you so.'"

He grinned. "Yeah, I love to say 'I told you so.' It's

one of my favorite things. No, stay up there a minute," he said when she started to dismount. "I want to check something out."

So saying, he put his hand on her thigh, keeping his touch carefully impersonal. She stiffened.

"Relax," he said curtly. "I need to know how the joints are working together." He moved her leg farther back, studying the way the movement affected the hip and spine. "When you took the fall that broke your wrist, where else did you hit?"

"My hip. But there wasn't any real damage, just one heck of a bruise."

He nodded. "The muscles are still stiff, though, aren't they? You compensated beautifully, but I..." He looked up as he spoke. She was staring at him, her pleasure-swelled pupils making her eyes darker, deeper. Delicate color washed her cheeks. "I prescribe extra stretches," he finished quickly, dropping his hand.

Dammit, he was screwing up again. He wanted to make Maggie feel desirable. He didn't want to seduce her.

Or did he? Did he even know what he wanted? "Inspection's over." He angled his body away to hide his reaction, running a hand along the mare's neck, murmuring to her.

Maggie dismounted. "She's pretty patient in the arena for such a young horse."

"She's lively, but she likes to please. If you feed her plenty of praise, she'll do just about anything for you." Maybe he was fooling himself when he thought he could do right by Maggie. For damned sure he wouldn't be able to stay out of her bed if she kept looking at him the way she had just now. Giving the horse a last pat, he turned back to Maggie. "When you were wandering around the house making Sarita suspicious, did you see the training room?''

"Ah—I don't think so. What's the training room?"

"The one with the mats, weights and other instruments of torture."

"No, I didn't. Wait." She put the back of her hand to her forehead and rolled her eyes dramatically. "I'm having a psychic moment. I see…crunches. Many, many crunches in my future."

"Among other things." He started walking, heading for the small field where he usually turned out the horses after working them. "What's your off-season regimen?"

"Crunches, squats, light weights." She unfastened her helmet, took it off and ran her fingers through her hair. "In-season, I do a lot more, of course. Walt was big on building upper-body strength. He said that was my weakest point."

He snorted. "Hitchcock thinks women are small, deformed men. You do need strength in your arms and shoulders, but knowing him, I'll bet he was trying to turn you into an inferior sort of male instead of working with your strengths as a woman."

Her eyebrows lifted. "I didn't know I had any strengths as a woman—as a female athlete, I mean."

"Your center of balance is lower, so you have a natural balance in the saddle a man has to work to earn. Most of your strength is in your legs and hips, right where a rider needs it. Then, too, women are more likely to think their way through a situation instead of trying to muscle it out, so you learn to ride with your brain as well as your body."

"Wow. You sure you're the same sex as Walt?"

"Last time I checked." A risqué comment rose to his lips, but he swallowed it. He'd seen Maggie's face back at the stable, when she'd hinted that she'd be willing to come to his bed, if necessary, to make their marriage more credible.

Yeah, he'd screwed up, all right. Maggie wanted him. And that was going to make everything a great deal harder than he'd anticipated.

At the unwitting mental pun, he smiled ruefully.

"Share the joke?"

"Not this time. Let's get her back to the stable." He started walking, letting her lead the horse. "How did the saddle feel?"

"Too big. I'm going to need my saddles, and the rest of my gear. For that matter, I'm going to need my truck. Maybe Ed can take me into Dallas to get my things."

"I'll take you. Can you wait until the weekend?"

"Oh, but you...you're busy. One of the hands can take me."

"Afraid of the fireworks if we run into your father?"

"Yes," she said honestly.

"I won't provoke him." With luck, he wouldn't have to. Luke opened the big double door. Maggie and Gotcha Girl followed. The horse looked eager, no doubt anticipating the flakes of hay waiting for her in her stall.

The woman looked wary. "He's going to be provoked the second I walk in the door. Seeing you will just make it worse."

"So maybe he'll pick on me instead of you." He hoped so. That would give him all the excuse he needed. "I'm going with you, Maggie."

"All right." She sighed, opened the stall door and let the mare inside. "Maybe we could pick up a tree while we're out."

"A tree?" He smiled, amused, as he loosened the

girth. "Don't you think there are enough trees around here?"

"A Christmas tree," she said patiently. "You know, one of those things that shed needles all over? It's nearly December, and I like to get the tree up early so I can enjoy it longer. We'll need some decorations, too. I have a few of my own, but—what's wrong?"

"I don't do Christmas." He pulled the saddle from the mare's back and started for the tack room.

"You don't—hey, wait up." She grabbed his arm. "What do you mean, you don't do Christmas? Not at all? I know you're not Jewish."

"I mean no tinsel or holly. No tree with lights, no cards, no carols, no stockings."

"Well, I do Christmas. Lights, a tree, packages, the whole bit."

"Not at my house, you don't."

He saw the hurt flash through her eyes, and cursed himself. He could have been more pleasant. But she drew herself up to her full five foot two and a half, squared her shoulders and said firmly. "Luke, Christmas is important to me. I won't hang tinsel from the chandeliers since you don't celebrate the season yourself, but I want a tree."

He looked at her stubborn chin and uncertain eyes, thought about her antiwuss campaign and sighed. "You picked a bad subject to practice standing up for yourself, Maggie. Let it go."

She put her hands on her hips. "Why the Grinch act? I don't get it."

But she ought to. She was the one person in the world who should understand why he hated Christmas...but it had been nine years, hadn't it? A long time. Long enough that he couldn't call his seasonal moodiness grief. Maggie might not even remember what had happened on that Christmas Eve so many years ago…abruptly, he moved away. "If you can't live without some of the holiday trappings, you can have a tree in your room."

He went to the tack room and put up the saddle and pad. She followed and hung the breastplate and bridle on their pegs. "This sucks."

"Life does, sometimes."

"My mother always gets professionals in to do the tree and everything. The only time I've ever been able to decorate for Christmas myself was during my brief fling with independence, right after college. And then I was too broke to do much."

"You had a little trouble with employment, as I recall."

She grinned suddenly. "Oh, a lot of trouble, I'd say. Six jobs in eighteen months is a bit much."

"Six?" He shook his head. "I know about the one at MacAdams ranch—didn't blame you for quitting that bastard. But as I recall, you argued with the owner of Belrose stables, too, when you worked there."

"But he was wrong! He wanted me to use a gadget bit to correct problems that should have been addressed with more thorough training, and he *forbade* me to work any of his horses without a martingale. Can you believe that? Now, I'm not saying there aren't horses or situations where a martingale might be appropriate, but to refuse to train without them when any fool can see—"

Luke held his hands up, laughing. "Okay, okay. I see why you argued with him. Where was it you ended up after that? Some kind of store, wasn't it?"

"A jewelry store." She sighed. "Do you have any idea how much those places mark up their stuff?"

Fascinated, he asked, "Did you by any chance mention the markup to the customers?"

"Of course not. All I did was suggest that this nice young couple might do better at one of the big chain stores, where they don't have such a steep markup. They didn't have much money, Luke."

"I suppose your boss didn't sympathize with your noble motives. There was some kind of secretarial job, too, wasn't there?"

"At a law firm. I was completely unsuited for it—all that professional decorum and wearing panty hose and sitting at a desk. Yech. I don't know why they hired me."

"I'm guessing it was a man who hired you."

"Well yeah, but that didn't have anything to do with it. Mr. McKinney was a nice old fellow, not a roving hands artist. *That* was my boss at the planetarium." She shook her head. "Who would have thought a scientific type would be such a lech?"

She didn't have a clue, did she? She truly had no idea how she affected men. "That's five jobs. What was the sixth?"

"The biggest mistake of all. I worked for my father for two months." She shuddered. "Otherwise known as the months from hell."

"Hey. You cussed."

"Did I?" Her brow wrinkled. "I'm not sure that counts. 'Hell' is in the Bible, after all."

"So's 'damn,' and I'm pretty sure that's a cuss word."

"So it is." Her voice lifted in surprise. "And I said it without even thinking."

She looked so pleased with herself, he had to grin. He flicked her cheek with one finger. "C'mon, Maggie, do it again. Talk dirty to me."

"Idiot."

''I'm getting excited already.''

''Stuff it, you oversexed poster boy.''

''That's good, but still G-rated. Instead of 'stuff it,' you should tell me to stick it—''

''Where the sun don't shine,'' she finished, laughing. ''Come on, Luke. Let's brush poor Gotcha Girl.''

They did. Luke's suggestions for increasing her cussing grew more outrageous while they worked together until, her cheeks crimson, she retaliated by dumping a half-full bucket of grain over his head. He laughed and made her clean it up.

By the time Maggie headed back to the house to do the prescribed exercises, Luke was feeling better than he had all day. He whistled cheerfully as he led out a promising gelding he'd just begun training.

He hadn't lost Maggie. In spite of everything, they were still friends. And as long as he kept his hands off her, they would stay that way.

Six

It was going to be seduction, after all.

Maggie pulled the brush through her hair and brooded over the sheer contrariness of the man she was more or less married to. After kissing her silly that first night, then teasing and tantalizing her the next day, Luke had either lost interest or suffered a pang of conscience. He hadn't touched her since. Oh, she'd tried hinting, and he was always ready with a quick, flirtatious comeback—but it was the don't-take-this-seriously kind of flirting. Like when he'd told her to "talk dirty" to him.

How could a woman let a man know she wanted him when he treated the very idea of sex between them as a joke?

Maggie tossed the brush on the bed. Hard.

Today they were driving into Dallas to pick up her gear, her horse trailer and truck and whatever else she might need for the next few months. And today, once she had her truck, she was going to Victoria's Secret to buy a couple of sexy nightgowns.

And just what did she do then? she asked herself as she left her room. Parade around the house in a few scraps of satin and lace and hope he mistakes her goose bumps for breasts and is swept away by lust?

Maybe she should level with him. *By the way, Luke, I was hoping you could train me in something other than riding. Mind if we go to bed so you can make a woman out of me?*

Maggie shuddered. Better hope he's crazy about goose bumps.

She glanced at her watch. Two-forty, and Luke had said they'd leave at three, so she had time to get something to eat. She'd been too busy for lunch, so she was running on empty.

She headed for the kitchen.

Sarita was there. She'd abandoned her suspicious reserve after the first day, having apparently decided Maggie was more in need of guidance than guarding. "You'll eat before you go," she said firmly. "Sit down. I saved some of the enchiladas from last night so you could have a hot meal, and then you didn't come in for lunch."

"I'm here now," Maggie said meekly, sitting at the table while Sarita put a plate in the microwave. "Tell me something. Don't you find it awkward to mother someone who's three years older than you?"

"I am a married lady." Sarita slid the steaming plate in front of Maggie. "This gives me a perspective you lack."

Maggie glanced at the ring on her right hand. "Oh?"

"Oh, that." She made a dismissive noise and sat across from Maggie, tossing her yard of black hair over her shoulder. "You have a ring, but sleeping in separate beds on opposite sides of the house is *not* married."

"I don't know when I've met anyone so preoccupied with my sex life." Maggie scooped up a forkful of the spicy enchiladas and savored the steamy scent. "I don't suppose it would do any good to tell you it's none of your business?"

"You always change the subject," she said severely. "You're as bad as Luke. Every time I ask him why he lets you sleep alone, he gets sillier."

"You ask him?" Fascinated, Maggie put down her fork. "Frequently?"

"If I don't ask, how will I learn what I want to know?"

"What does he say?"

"Oh, nonsense." Sarita spread her arms wide to indicate how large his nonsense was. "That it's none of my business, that you snore, that he's taken a vow of celibacy. Fa!"

Fa was Sarita's all-purpose exclamation, used for anger, disgust, any of the emotions that drove most people to cursing. Maggie was considering adopting it. "Why does it matter so much to you?" she asked curiously.

"I like Luke."

"I do, too. But why are you so worried about our, ah, sleeping arrangements?"

Sarita paused, giving the question serious consideration. "He's a good man," she said at last. "But just a man, so he's also a fool. All those women of his—this one, that one, another next week—he thinks he's a bumblebee with a big field of flowers to pollinate. I can see this is bad for him, but what man will believe one woman is best? He needs a good woman to show him, or he'll still be playing with the flowers when he is old and sad."

She leaned forward. ''Luke, he is a man who needs children.''

Maggie opened her mouth to say that she'd never seen Luke show any desire to father children—and closed it again. Until this past week, that might have been true. But she'd seen him with his students.

They were troubled kids. Boys with a single parent, or none at all. Boys who, although young—the oldest was a bright, hostile twelve-year-old named Jeremy—were already in trouble. The Big Brothers organization was involved in some way, though Maggie wasn't clear on the details; Luke was remarkably closemouthed about the whole thing.

And he was nuts about those boys. ''He really loves working with those hellions of his, doesn't he?''

''You've seen it, then? The way he comes alive with the boys? Especially that Jeremy. He needs children of his own. Eat,'' she said, getting up from the table. ''You don't want me to be insulted, do you? Eat your lunch.''

Maggie grinned and went back to eating, but, however delicious, Sarita's enchiladas couldn't hold her attention.

Was Sarita right? Did Luke long for children of his own?

It seemed far-fetched. Luke was, to put it bluntly, a womanizer. Maggie liked him. She lusted after him. She had even, at one time, fancied herself in love with him. But she wasn't blind to his faults. Still, just because a man had a weakness for women in the plural didn't mean he couldn't be a good father, or that he didn't want children. But it was hard to picture Luke pining away for children of his own.

Although...

She bit her lip. An image floated into her mind, a memory of Luke's face nine years ago. A spectacular face,

young and strong, with cheekbones any model would
envy. And tears running down those elegant cheeks.

She made a small noise—of startlement, discovery,
confusion. Sarita, at the dishwasher, looked over her
shoulder. "What? The enchiladas are too hot?"

"No, they're great." Sarita knew Luke, cared about
him. Maggie was strongly tempted to ask if she knew
about the baby that hadn't lived to be born.

No, she decided. Luke wouldn't have told Sarita. He
never spoke of what had happened, and he'd hate it if
Maggie said anything. "I'm going to buy some nightgowns," she blurted instead.

"Nightgowns?" Sarita's thin eyebrows flew up like
mobile parentheses enclosing her surprise. "What do you
want with nightgowns? Naked is better."

"Never mind," Maggie said, embarrassed beyond
words. She shoved her chair back.

"Sexy nightgowns, though…" Sarita considered that,
then nodded. "It's a start."

When Maggie stepped outside, the sun was a bright,
hard ball in a blazingly blue sky, and the air was fresh
and calm and cool. Good thing it had warmed up some
the past couple of days, she thought as she headed for
the truck. Her leather jacket was staying behind, and she
hated to be cold.

Luke was waiting in his truck. He leaned across to
open the door for her. "Hello. My name is Luke West.
And you are—?"

She gave him a quizzical look as she climbed in. "I
think the minister used our names in Vegas."

"Yeah, but you don't look like Maggie." He put the
truck in gear and started down the long driveway. "Don't
get me wrong. You look great. But not like Maggie."

She glanced down at the dark green sweater she'd worn over an oxford-style shirt, the slacks she'd taken the time to press, and sighed. "These are my 'good girl' clothes. It's supposed to be an olive branch to my mother, but maybe I'm wimping out again."

"There's nothing wrong with trying to get along."

"But how do I know when I'm being mature about compromising, and when I'm selling out to keep the peace?"

He shrugged. "I'm hardly an expert on family relations. I know plenty about dealing with mothers, but it's all in the plural. I don't suppose it would help you much if I were to explain how to smooth things over when you run into the last stepmother while having lunch at the country club with the current one."

She tipped her head, curious. "You always speak of mothers in the plural. You never say much about your mother."

"The original model, you mean? Stephanie and I get along okay. She lives in Virginia—married to local politician there—so we don't see each other often. Not that we saw all that much of each other before."

She looked for bitterness, but couldn't see any. Was he hiding it, playing things light the way he so often did? Or was he truly not bitter over the way his mother had relinquished custody to his father when he was a boy? "Obviously you aren't close. What about your stepmothers? Are you close to any of them?"

"I've stayed in touch with Kaylene. She's a good-natured sort, fun to be around—and not all that much older than I am," he added wryly. "Then there's Felicia."

He fell silent as soon as he'd spoken that name, and his eyes looked sad. Maggie hesitated, then decided to try Sarita's philosophy: if you want to know, ask. "Which one was she?"

"Michael's mother. Mostly my father managed to pick resilient women. Felicia...wasn't. She did try to be a mother to us, but she wasn't up to the challenge posed by the West males. After the divorce...well, I don't know which came first, the drink or the despair, but she's been in and out of treatment centers for years. We all sort of look out for her."

She absorbed the information in silence. It was no surprise to learn that Jacob helped care for one of his stepmothers. The oldest West brother might be intimidating, but you could put his picture in the dictionary next to "responsible." But Luke took pains to seem just the opposite—passionate about his riding, undependable everywhere else.

At last she said, "Did anyone ever tell you you're a nice guy?"

"Nice?" He gave her one of those easy, sexy smiles. "I hear stupendous, incredible, and 'oh, my God' a lot, but I don't think anyone has mentioned nice."

"I'm not talking about sex." She frowned impatiently. "I mean you're *nice*. Helping take care of Michael's mom...then there's what you're doing for Ada. And those boys you teach—"

"For God's sake, don't start giving me all sorts of noble motives. I like working with the boys, or I wouldn't do it. I'm still the selfish SOB you've always known."

"Okay." She wouldn't argue with him, since the very idea that he might be genuinely nice embarrassed him. But her picture of Luke was changing, and she wasn't sure she was comfortable with the changes. This warmth that spread in her middle when she thought about Luke's commitment to his boys might be as alluring as the soft center of a Godiva truffle, but she had to protect herself. Better to think of Luke the way he did himself—as charming, selfish, inconstant.

And he was inconstant. She needed to remember that.

For the rest of the way into Dallas, they talked casually about the ranch and Luke's horses. They were navigating the huge concrete pretzel south of Balch Springs, a Dallas suburb, when Luke referred to his boys again.

"Once we get your things loaded," he said, switching lanes smoothly, "would you mind if we swing by Jeremy's place? He, ah, stays at the ranch some weekends, does some chores in exchange for extra lessons."

"Sure, no problem." So the boy would be staying with them the whole weekend? That went well beyond the casually selfish interest Luke insisted he took in his students. It also put paid to any vague notions she'd had about parading around the house in a sexy negligee. "Jeremy is the one who scowls a lot so his dimples won't show, right?"

"That's him. You beat the record for getting a real smile out of him, by the way. He usually won't let out anything but scowls or smirks until he's known someone a month or so."

"He's cute. Not that I'd be fool enough to tell him so."

"If you did, he'd probably hit on you."

"Luke!" Shocked, she twisted in her seat to look at him. "He's only twelve."

"He's not like the kids you're used to, Maggie."

"If you're referring to the fact that he's a mixed-race child—"

"I'm talking about the way he's lived, not his genetic code. He's got an uncle doing hard time. His mother was beaten to death by one of her johns. Not that I'm criticizing her. She did the best for him she could. She was fourteen when she got pregnant, fifteen when her mother threw her and her baby out on the streets. Somehow, through sheer guts, love, threats—whatever—she kept Jeremy out of the gangs.''

Maggie couldn't speak. There was a trace of shame in even trying to imagine what the boy's life had been like. It made her feel small and petty. How often had she complained about her own upbringing? ''What happened to him after his mother died?''

''His grandmother wouldn't take him in and they couldn't find his aunt, so he got tossed into the foster care system. The first family he was placed with tossed him right back—called him incorrigible.'' His mouth tightened. ''Jeremy's got a bellyful of rage, but he's not a lost cause.''

''How did you wind up teaching him riding?''

''He did get lucky in one way. His social worker is one of the best. She found out that he'd always wanted to ride, and she knew I'd been working with some boys through Big Brothers. She set it up.''

''He's a good rider.'' She'd seen him on the quarter horse Luke kept for lessons. ''He's got a good seat and a real feel for moving with the horse. Tries to control the horse with the bit too much, though.''

''He sat on a horse for the first time in his life ten months ago.''

''You're kidding! I took him for having, oh—two or three years of lessons.''

There was a hint of pride in his voice. ''Jeremy eats, sleeps and dreams horses. There is nothing in the world he wants more than to ride. He's got a shot at being world-class—if the Pearsons don't screw it up for him.''

''Who are they?''

"His current foster family. Good people, I suppose," Luke said grudgingly. "They keep a close watch on him, and Lord knows he needs it. As long as he keeps up with his schoolwork and stays out of trouble, they've said he can continue his lessons. But they don't encourage him. They worry that he's setting his goals too high, that he'll be disappointed. They say they can't afford all the expenses that go with competing. Dammit, no one's asking them to! I *can* afford it. They don't have to."

"You're planning to sponsor him?" she asked, startled. "How far?"

"As far as he wants to go. It's no big deal, Maggie. Trainers trade lessons for stable work all the time."

Lessons, yeah. But they didn't include tack, entrance fees, transport and road expenses in the deal, much less a horse. A seasoned event horse could cost as much as a new car. "You're going to mount him for competition?"

"If he goes that far. For now, he'll be working with Samson. Jeremy wants to jump, of course," Luke said, turning off on a residential street. "I'm using that as the carrot to get him to do the basic dressage work he needs. He's eager to try cross-country, too, the rougher the better—it's more macho than arena work." He chuckled. "But he needs a lot more training and experience first."

She nodded. Samson was a good choice—a big, patient warmblood with impeccable manners and a strong sense of stubborn, he'd teach the boy as much as Luke would. Samson would do anything you asked of him, but you had to ask correctly.

"We're almost there," Luke said. "You haven't called your mother to let her know you're coming, have you?"

Guilt itched up her spine. "So I'm a coward. It's Friday. My father will be at work—unless Mom calls and tells him I'm coming, and he decides to show up so he can explain my faults to me.''

"Hmm." Luke was silent as he turned off on her street. "Looks like you were worrying for nothing," he said after a moment. "Your mother won't need to notify your father. That's his car in the driveway."

She rang the bell. It struck Luke as wrong, somehow. He didn't think he'd ever used the doorbell at the house that used to be his father's and now belonged to Jacob. If he had, of course, Ada would have given him a hard time about it, fussing that he'd be making her traipse all over the house just to let him in.

He frowned at the evergreen wreath on the door. Maggie had said her mother always had professionals handle the holiday decorating, and the wreath did have a professional look—tasteful and expensive, like the multitude of tiny white lights strung in the bare limbs of the live oaks. Just the sort of thing you expected to find in a neighborhood like this, and not at all what Maggie would enjoy.

What kind of decorations would she have inflicted on his house if he'd let her? Something loud and cheerful and borderline tacky, he suspected.

He was smiling slightly when the door opened.

"Miss Maggie!" The woman who opened the door was dressed in housekeeper gray that matched the beauty-shop curls on her head. "Don't you look a picture! This must be Luke. Mr. West, I mean." She beamed at them. "I was *that* happy when I heard—oh, listen to me. I didn't mean to run on and keep you standing in the cold." She stepped aside. "Your parents are in the living room. They'll be so glad to see you."

If Maggie had any doubts about that, she didn't mention them as she went inside. Luke followed.

The holiday hadn't been allowed to intrude on the muted colors and antiques of the foyer, unless the bowl of red and green apples on the Sheraton table was a nod to the season. The bowl itself was silver, and highly polished; white candles with pristine wicks flanked it. There were two elegant straight-backed chairs facing the table that Luke felt sure no one ever sat in.

It all made him want to kick his boots off in the middle of the spotless floor, or straddle one of those unused chairs. Do something, anything, to mess up the pretty perfection of the place.

"Luke, this is Marilyn," Maggie said. "She holds things together around here. Marilyn, you guessed it. This is my—ah, my husband, Lucas West."

"I'm delighted to meet you, sir."

Luke murmured something appropriate, but his attention was on Maggie. She all but vibrated with tension, like a wire strung too tight. Was it really that hard for her to face her father?

"Shall I take your jacket?" Marilyn asked him.

He would rather have tossed it over the newel post at the foot of the stairs, but surrendered it without protest. He wasn't here to cause trouble.

Not unless Malcolm Stewart insisted on trouble, that is.

The maid left down a short hall. He and Maggie had started for the living room when Sharon Stewart's voice reached them.

"It's been a week," she said. "I just want to call and make sure she's all right."

"Absolutely not," Malcolm Stewart said crisply. "We will not cater to her freakish behavior by contacting her.

When she realizes what a mistake she's made, she'll come home.''

Maggie stopped short of the doorway, so Luke did, too. He took her elbow and looked a question at her. He didn't have any moral objections to a little eavesdropping, but she might not like what she heard.

She didn't even see him. Her entire attention was on what was being said in the room just ahead of them. He slipped an arm around her. She glanced at him then, startled.

Her mother was speaking in a soft, doubting voice. ''Margaret can be very stubborn. What if she doesn't come home?''

''She'll be back. When she runs out of money, she won't have any choice.'' There was the chinking sound of ice being dropped in a glass. ''My brother called me today. He asked about Margaret.''

''Oh, dear. I knew there would be rumors. I just knew it.''

''Then you shouldn't have confided in Amelia Bretton. For God's sake, Sharon, show some sense once in a while.''

Luke glanced at Maggie. She grimaced, but when he tried to urge her forward, she resisted.

''I'm sure Amelia didn't repeat anything I told her! She promised not to.''

''Nonetheless, the story is out, and as a result I had a thoroughly unpleasant conversation with my brother. He wanted to know if Margaret had indeed run off with the—well, I shall edit his language. He was heated. I can't blame him. Luke West ruined his daughter's life.''

That was one way of looking at it. Luke's mouth twisted.

''Oh, but ruined is such a harsh word, and Pamela

seems...though I do wish she would settle down, but that's neither here nor there. Malcolm, do you think we should send a notice about the marriage to the papers? If rumors are already spreading—''

''Do try to think, dear. They didn't get married. The only reason a man like him marries is if he's drunk or his hand is forced.''

The shoulders beneath Luke's arm tensed.

''But he did ask her,'' Sharon offered timidly. ''I heard him. There was no force involved.''

An impatient sigh. ''I was referring to the remote possibility that West had married her because he got her pregnant.''

''Oh, no. No, I don't think so. There was nothing loverlike in the way they acted with each other.''

''For once I agree with you. I've no doubt West could talk himself into Margaret's bed if he wished, but why would he bother? Oh, for heaven's sake, don't look so distressed. Margaret is lovely in our eyes, naturally, but she is hardly the type to attract a man like him. No, I suspect she arranged the whole little drama for our benefit, and West went along because it amused him. She's punishing us. She wants us to believe she ran off with him, when in truth she's hiding somewhere, sulking over not getting her way.''

Luke had heard more than enough. ''Not exactly,'' he called out cheerfully. ''In fact,'' he said as he used the arm around Maggie to bring her into the room with him, ''you're wrong on pretty much every count.''

Out of the corner of his eyes he could see that Maggie's face was flaming, but mostly he was looking at the two slim, well-bred people staring at him with such different expressions. Maggie's mother looked appalled. Her father was furious.

"Eavesdropping, West?" he said with icy courtesy.

"What can you expect from a man like me?" He shook his head sadly. "Only the worst. Still, you've managed to jump to all the wrong conclusions. First…" He squeezed Maggie's shoulder and gave her a fond look. "We *are* married. And Maggie isn't even pregnant. Amazing, isn't it?"

"Luke," Maggie whispered, "if this is your idea of not making trouble, I have to say you don't seem to get the idea."

He hushed her with a quick kiss—very quick, to keep the low buzz of desire from shooting up and redlining his brain. "Second…well, maybe I can't blame a daddy for not realizing his little girl has grown up into a woman who makes men drool, so I'll tuck my tongue back in my mouth and assure you that Maggie is definitely my kind of woman."

He was appreciating the mingling of anger and alarm on Stewart's face so much he didn't notice when Sharon stepped forward until her husband said sharply, "Sharon."

She hesitated, looking from him to her daughter, her expression as anxious as a rabbit staring down a hunter's gun barrel. But then she squared her shoulders and crossed the room, stopping in front of Luke. She held out both hands to him. "In that case," she said with quiet dignity, "welcome to our family, Luke."

Seven

"That went really well, don't you think?" Maggie said as she passed him a pillowcase full of odds and ends.

Luke stood in the bed of the truck. They'd forgotten to pick up boxes, so most of Maggie's worldly goods were stashed in three large trash bags and the pillowcase she'd just handed him. Her saddles and tack, of course, wouldn't be treated so cavalierly. They were in the custom horse trailer her father had given her for her twenty-first birthday. "Define 'well,'" he said dryly as he vaulted over the side of the truck.

"No one took a swing at anyone."

"In that case—yeah, I'd say it went great." He headed for the driver's side of the truck. "Time to get the trailer hooked up. Get the garage door open, will you?"

She did that. Her parents' garage was as large as the one at Jacob's house, with room for several cars—and at one end, an RV-sized addition for Maggie's fancy horse trailer. She gave him elaborate ''come on'' gestures as he backed the truck up.

She started chattering again as soon as he got out. ''I couldn't believe it when my mother crossed the room like that and held out her hands to you. Weren't you surprised? Father didn't want her to, either. But she did it anyway.''

''Yeah.'' She was so excited by her mother's small show of support. Something soft and aching spread through him. He wanted to gather her up and hold her. Just hold her. ''She did it for your sake. Hey, quit that!''

She was cranking the handle on the trailer's tongue, ratcheting it up. ''I only have one broken arm. This one works fine. See?'' She flashed him a grin. ''Make yourself useful and back your truck up a little more.''

It didn't take long to get the trailer hitched up. He had to admit she behaved herself then, letting him load her saddles.

''Thanks for coming with me,'' she said, as he stowed the last of her gear. ''If I gave the impression earlier that I didn't want you to—''

''You did.''

''I thought you'd make everything worse. And at first it seemed like you would. The things you said to my father—!'' She chuckled. ''For a minute there, I thought you were going to ravish me on the spot to make your point.''

He finished securing the trailer door. ''I never ravish for an audience.''

''What about orgies?''

''What?''

''Orgies aren't exactly doing it *for* an audience—they're doing it *with* the audience. Have you ever—''

''Good Lord, Maggie, what a question!''

''I'm trying out Sarita's technique—if you want to know, ask.''

He shook his head in disbelief. ''And you want to know if I've ever participated in group sex?''

''Um.'' She thought that over. ''Maybe not. I guess the corollary to Sarita's theory would be, 'If you don't want to know, don't ask.''''

He started laughing. ''I'll say one thing for you—you keep me on my toes. I never know what you're going to say next. If I'd known marriage could be so entertaining, I've have tried it years ago.'' As soon as he realized what he'd said, his laughter faded.

He had tried marriage once, years ago.

Maggie sighed, her mind apparently going down the same track his had. ''I'm sorry about what my father said about your ruining Pamela's life. He's pretty blind where she's concerned. It's those eyelashes of hers, I think. Then, too, she cries really well.''

Reluctantly his mouth kicked up. Pamela *had* cried well, her big blue eyes shimmering with distress, the tears pooling, then spilling. Sometimes her bottom lip had quivered like a little girl's. At first her tears had made him feel protective. Later, they'd made him crazy. He'd run away from those tears night after night.

''Do you hate her?''

He turned away, heading for the pickup. ''She isn't important enough to me to hate.'' She never had been. That was the problem, the root of the whole, tawdry chain of events that had led to a tragedy no one but him seemed to remember anymore.

''Then it's because of the baby that you don't like Christmas?''

Her words jarred open the place inside where he never looked. Death twisted through him—empty, endlessly and forever empty, a hole dug by guilt and grief at the bottom of his soul. He reached for the pickup's door, his fingers tight on the handle, pulling himself away from that sucking hole. "Shut up, Maggie."

"Okay. But it might help to talk about it. You never do, but if you're still miserable at Christmas after all this time—"

"What I don't need," he said, his voice as tight as his jaws, "is cheap psychobabble about talking things out. Go on, get in your car. I'll see you back at the ranch."

She fell silent then, thank God. Once he could ease his attention away from the memories, it was almost as if the hole didn't exist. He yanked open the door.

His cell phone rang. He grabbed it from the seat without getting in.

The conversation was short, and did nothing to improve his mood. When he disconnected Maggie was still there, watching him with an odd expression on her face. "What are you staring at?"

"Your shoulders, mostly. I gather that was about Jeremy?"

His shoulders? What the hell did that mean? "Yeah. His foster mother found out he had a school project he's supposed to work on with some other kids tonight. He hadn't told her, or she would have called me sooner. The upshot is that he can't come out to the ranch until tomorrow. I'm supposed to pick him up about noon."

"That's a shame." She seemed occupied with some interior matter. "You'll have to drive all the way into Dallas again tomorrow, then."

"No, I think I'll just stay here tonight." The thought gave him a measure of relief. The past few nights had been hard as hell...literally. Knowing Maggie was in the house, in bed—accessible—had kept him awake too often. A night away from her would do him good.

"You'll what? Stay here in Dallas?"

He had her full attention now. His eyebrows went up. "You have a problem with that?"

"No. That is, not exactly. How about if I stay here with you?"

Hell, no. "What's going on, Maggie? You don't trust me alone in the big city overnight?"

"No, no. That's not it. I just, ah…" She bit her lip. Looked at her shoes, at the trailer, at the sky. "Well, heck." At last she met his eyes, offering a candid smile. "This is embarrassing. The thing is, I thought I'd be following you back to the ranch. I'm nervous about driving back by myself."

"You're what?" He shook his head slowly. "That doesn't wash, Maggie. You've driven cross-country to events with no one but Dandy for company." Anger steamed up inside, making his voice hard. "If you don't think I can keep my word for one night—"

"No!" She grabbed his arm, but snatched her hand back immediately. "That isn't it, truly. It's, ah—it's this arm." She waved her cast to indicate which arm she meant. "I can drive with it, but it feels awkward. I've got a manual transmission, you know—better for hauling that trailer around. But of course I can hold on to the steering wheel with my left hand long enough to shift gears. No problem there," she assured him, as if he'd questioned it. "But if something happened—say I got a flat. I can't jack the truck up myself, can I?"

"No, but…" He frowned, studying her. She was hiding something. Damned if he could figure out what it was, but her bright smile looked more relieved than embarrassed.

"Never mind," she said cheerfully. "I'm being silly. What could go wrong? If I get a flat or have car trouble, I'll just pull over to the side of the road and wait for someone to help me."

"No, you won't! You'll roll up your windows and lock your doors and use your cell phone to call for help."

"Okay. Whatever you say, although I think—but it doesn't matter. I'm sure I won't have car trouble." She waved the cast again. "Forget I said anything. I'll be fine on the highway by myself."

He didn't trust her. When Maggie said "okay" that way, she meant she'd rather not argue. It didn't have anything to do with actually agreeing. "You'd better wait until tomorrow to go back," he said abruptly.

"I don't think—"

"Sometimes that's true. I'm not taking a chance of you relying on 'the kindness of strangers' if you have a flat. I'll follow you to the ranch tomorrow just to make sure."

"Well…" She heaved a sigh. "All right, though I do feel foolish. Are we going to stay at Jacob's?"

"I…" He'd intended to, originally. But to stay there with Maggie…he frowned. She'd indicated she thought of his brother as a friend, but he didn't entirely buy that. And he felt sure Jacob hadn't seen her in that light. "Why don't you stay with one of your friends?"

She grimaced. "Oh, right. That would look great. I could explain that yes, I've just gotten married, and yes, Luke is in town, but we didn't want to spend the night together."

Dammit. He couldn't blame her for not wanting to deal with those kind of questions. His chance for a peaceful, restful night was fading fast. Grudgingly he conceded. "I guess I could get us rooms at the Sheraton on Douglas."

"That sounds good." She patted his arm. "Don't they

have VCRs? We can order in pizza and watch movies tonight. Doesn't that sound like fun? I'll pick some tapes up while I'm out.''

''Out?'' Somehow he'd lost control of the conversation. ''Where are you going?''

''Shopping.''

He glanced at the bed of his pickup. ''I think two out of three of those garbage bags hold clothes.''

''Oh, not for clothes. Just some girl stuff. And a couple movies, of course.'' Cheerfully she headed for her truck, a four-year-old Dodge Ram with new tires. ''Meet you at the hotel about seven, okay?''

He frowned. ''I thought you didn't want to drive around alone.''

''City driving doesn't bother me.'' She opened the door, climbed in and started the engine—which purred as if it had just been tuned.

Her window came down. She smiled reassuringly. ''Don't worry. I promise not to let anyone but ministers or mechanics help me if I have car trouble at the mall.''

The window went back up. Luke stood there and watched her back out of the garage, shaking his head. He'd just been had. He was sure of that. But for the life of him, he couldn't figure out what she was up to.

Eight

It had been amazingly easy to get Luke to insist she stay in Dallas overnight. Maggie felt guilty for tricking him, but desperate women took desperate measures.

Her plan had come to her in a flash when he'd said he would stay in Dallas overnight. She'd known this was her chance. They would have pizza together in her hotel room—on the bed, because where else was there to sit in comfort? Surely once she had him in bed—or on the bed—she could take it from there. Luke's libido was notoriously easy to excite.

It had worked before. Not that she had intended it to, that time. She hadn't known she'd run into Luke in the bar last December. Well, maybe she should have guessed that was possible—they'd both attended the horse show in Phoenix, after all. She'd seen him there, talked to him for a few minutes. But she hadn't known he was staying in the same hotel she was, or that they'd end up in her room, watching old movies on TV. She hadn't had a clue that he wanted her...

He hadn't, she reminded herself briskly. Not really. He'd been tipsy, and what he'd done had been instinct. Or habit. It wasn't his fault she'd felt a lot more than a quick physical rush, that she'd thought a barely acknowledged dream was coming true.

Maggie shook her head, annoyed with herself. She needed to fine-tune her plan, not wallow in a past folly. What if a cuddle on the bed didn't get Luke's instincts to take over? He wouldn't be tipsy this time. She'd probably have to do something...put her hand on his chest, maybe. Or his thigh. Whatever. She'd figure it out. She'd never seduced anyone, but how hard could it be? Especially with Luke.

She frowned at the rest of her plan—the two nightgowns tossed across the hotel bed. One was shimmery black-satin sin that ended a breath below scandal, with wisps of lace to cup the breasts. There was a robe to go with it, but it was too short to hide much.

She might be desperate, she decided, but she didn't want to look that way. Luke would know what was on her mind the second he saw her in that nightgown.

And what would he do then? Pounce on her? Laugh? Look at her with pity, and apologetically turn her down?

She shuddered and undressed quickly, then reached for the other gown she'd bought. It was cotton, not satin, a soft, stretchy knit. Red, yes, but not a siren-red. Rather Christmassy, she thought. And it was long. It went all the way to the floor. The sleeves were short, the better to get them over her cast. All in all, it looked more like a really long T-shirt than a nightgown.

Perfect. It would make him wonder what was on her

mind without jumping to any unpleasantly accurate conclusions.

Once she pulled it on, though, it didn't fit like any of
her T-shirts. She studied herself in the mirror over the
dresser. The bright green cast looked Christmassy next
to the red gown, but more silly than seductive. Well,
there was no getting around that. The gown itself was a
bit snug here and there. Especially *there.* Beneath the
clinging fabric her breasts were...obvious.

Too obvious. Panic clutched her stomach. She couldn't
do this. She'd make a fool of herself.

She'd started to tug the gown off when there was a
knock at her door. "Yes," she said, her voice muffled
by cloth. The dratted thing was stuck on her cast.

"The pizza showed up ten minutes ago and you didn't,
so I brought it to you."

Luke.

She took a deep breath and pulled the gown back in
place. "Right," she called. *I can, too, do this,* she told
herself as she started for the door. She had to. "I got the
movies," she said, opening the door. He stared. It was
gratifying, in a way. It was also horribly embarrassing.
"Uh—come in."

"I don't know if I should," he said slowly. "You're
not exactly dressed."

"Oh, I just wanted to get comfortable." Good thing
she hadn't worn the black satin, if red cotton had this—

Omigosh. The black, utterly obvious nightgown was
still on the bed.

"Come in!" she called again, but this time over her
shoulder as she dashed to the bed and scooped up the
incriminating nightie, thrusting it into the sack. But that
was a problem, too—the sack was unmistakably from
Victoria's Secret.

She glanced around frantically. And shoved the sack under the bed.

Luke had come into the room, but he hadn't closed the door behind him. He had a pizza box in one hand, two cans of soda in the other. And a puzzled frown on his face.

"That smells fantastic," she said brightly. "And you remembered the drinks. Great."

He gave her a strange, intent look—and kicked the door shut. He set the pizza down on the dresser. Then he came toward her, but there was something funny about the way he walked—loose, yet deliberate. Almost as if he were stalking her. He handed her one of the Cokes. "What movies did you rent?"

"That new one—the thriller with Brad Pitt? It's supposed to have great special effects. And, uh…" His voice had sounded normal. The way he popped open the soda and took a drink was as ordinary as could be. But his eyes, the way he was looking at her…*hot,* she realized. That was the word for it. His eyes were hot. And he wasn't smiling.

A little zip of alarm raced down her spine and settled in the pit of her stomach…where it didn't feel like alarm anymore.

"I've already seen it." His voice wasn't completely normal anymore. It was lower, more intimate. A little husky. "What else did you get?"

He was looking at her mouth. As if he were thinking about kissing her. Wanting to. *"Casablanca."*

"I've seen it, too." He stretched out one long arm and put his can of soda on the bedside table without taking his eyes from hers. The movement brought his body closer for a tantalizing moment, and her heartbeat kicked up.

"I-it's worth seeing again."

"Some things are," he agreed. His gaze drifted down. "You do know I can see the shape of your nipples through that material, don't you? They're hard."

After a second she closed her mouth with a little click of her teeth. "You don't—you can't—people don't *say* things like that!"

"I did." He touched the neckline of her gown, then ran his fingertips along it. "I can." The gown wasn't low. He wasn't touching her breasts. And she could scarcely breathe. "Why not?"

She took a step back. Her legs felt weak, undependable. There was a quivering at the tops of her thighs, heat in the pit of her stomach, and a tiny voice screaming inside her head that she was a fool. "Because it's embarrassing!"

His smile was slow and not especially friendly. "If you didn't want me to get ideas, Maggie, you shouldn't have slipped into that invitation you're wearing."

So much for making him wonder. But this was what she wanted, wasn't it? Everything was happening faster than she'd planned, but she could be flexible. Only why were his eyes so hard? She gulped down nerves and proceeded with her plan—flexibly. "Okay, you're right. I was thinking—well, we're married, more or less, so... why not?"

He just looked at her, his eyes hooded. She hadn't a clue what he was thinking, or what she was supposed to do next. She sure couldn't talk about nipples! Actions, she decided, spoke louder than words. She put her hand on his chest and smiled up at him. Seductively, she hoped.

He didn't move, but his eyes darkened. "Let me see

if I've got this right. You want to have sex? Now? Or after we eat?''

Her hand fell away. "Do you have to keep just saying everything out loud? Let me tell you, it's a lousy technique. You did better last time, when you'd been drinking.''

That startled him. "Last time? Is that what this is about? Are you trying to pay me back?''

"Pay you back?'' Outrage rose, making her forget she was humiliated. "For what? The most dismal night of my life? You think I *owe* you something for that?''

"No, dammit, I've been thinking for the past year that I owed you something! But maybe...'' His eyes narrowed. "My memory of that night is hazy. Maybe I've been beating myself up for nothing. Did you pull something like this that night in Phoenix, too?''

She stared. "You don't remember. You don't even remember.'' Abruptly she whirled around, grabbed his can of soda and shoved it at him. "Take your pizza and get out. I've lost my appetite.'' She glared at him and sniffed because she couldn't cry. *"All my appetites.''*

"Maggie.'' His voice was soft now. Gentle. It made her want to hit him. "I don't remember clearly because I was drunk.''

"You weren't,'' she insisted. "You'd had a few drinks, maybe, but your speech wasn't slurred and you walked just fine.'' He'd walked all the way to her hotel room that night...and out the door the next morning.

"I don't drink much. You know that, and you know why. I don't handle alcohol well. If I didn't seem drunk—well, chalk it up to an athlete's sense of balance. I was plastered. The gaps in my memory are from alcohol, not because you're unmemorable.''

She blinked rapidly. She couldn't cry. She never did;

she only got a runny nose, only—only she'd better turn
away, just in case.

So she did. "I told you to go. I've changed my mind."

"Have you?" He came up behind her. Fingers, warm
and callused, slid along her neck, rubbing lightly. "Are
you sure?"

"Y-yes." Why did she shiver? He was only touching
her neck. The bare skin of her neck. Lightly, his thumb
rubbing in small circles.

"Do you know how often I've wished I could remember that night better?" His hand left her neck to land just
above her waist. He stroked down her side—her waist,
her hip, the top of her thigh. "Almost as often as I've
worried about whether I damaged our friendship."

"There wasn't that much to remember," she muttered.

He laughed low in his throat. "That bad, was it?" He
put both hands on her shoulders and gently, firmly, pulled
her against him. Her breath caught. He was hard. All the
way hard and ready. She wanted to wiggle against that
enticing hardness.

Do it, she told herself. But if he rejected her again—
if his eyes got all cold and distant the way they had
before—

"Even without remembering much," he said, his
breath warm on her ear, "I've had a heck of a time keeping my hands off you. I've lain awake thinking about
doing…this."

This time he ran his hand up her stomach. Slowly. To
her ribs…until his thumb just touched the bottom of her
breast. Her head fell back against his shoulder.

"I want to," he whispered. "You can tell how much
I want to, can't you? But, sweetheart…" Gradually his
hand eased away, coming to rest at her waist again. "It

wouldn't be right. I don't want to hurt you, Maggie, not for anything."

"You won't," she whispered. "You can't." He'd cured her of that last year.

"I'm not going to risk it."

"*You're* not going to risk it?" Anger made her turn to face him. "Well—well—*damn!*" And she grabbed his face with her good hand and pulled his head down, going up on her tiptoes and aiming for his mouth.

She found it.

He didn't move. Whether he was stiff with shock, will-power or distaste, she didn't know. And in that moment she didn't care. She rubbed her mouth over his, and he tasted good. Wonderful. So she licked the closed line of his lips.

He shuddered. Then he grabbed her, yanked her up against him and took over. And she learned how little resemblance there was between kissing Luke drunk, and kissing him when he was sober.

His mouth was quick and demanding. His hands were hard and sure on her body, and oh, but he felt good, pressed up against her so tightly. A thrill raced up her spine. A needy ache set in to pulse between her legs.

But her stomach was tight. Deep in her belly anxiety crouched, cold and clenched and jittery, making her want to push him away. She could do that. He'd stop and she'd apologize, laugh at herself, make a joke of it—she could say she'd changed her mind, that he was right, she couldn't handle this, couldn't handle *him*—no. Determined not to let her fear win, she sent her hand racing over his back, his shoulders, cursing the cast that kept her from exploring him with both hands. Encouraging him to keep them both moving in the right direction.

He took direction well. One moment they were kissing,

mouths and tongues seeking, finding—the next she was flat on her back on the bed. He came down on top of her.

His mouth left hers to trail shivery kisses along the line of her neck, and she tilted her head, giving him better access. His leg came between hers and she gasped—and almost pulled away. The feelings were so strong, scary-strong. She wanted those feelings, wanted him, so badly.

What if she failed again?

No. No, she wouldn't let herself think of failure. Eager for the feelings he was bringing her to spread, to take over, she ran her hand up under his shirt, testing the muscles of his chest. *Take me there,* she pleaded with her silent mouth, with her touch. *Take me there quickly, before I mess this up.*

"Sugar," he said, nuzzling her ear, "unless you're in the mood for hard, hot and quick, we'd better slow down."

Sugar. He'd never called her that before. But he'd undoubtedly said it to plenty of women in situations just like this, with the two of them twined together in some bed.

Her hands stilled. And all those luscious, delightful feelings began to drain away, leaving only the fear, cold and sickly, oozing out from her stomach to her arms, her hands, her mind.

He kissed her again, slow and lingering. And raised his head, frowning down at her. "What's wrong?"

"Nothing." She made herself reach for him again, putting her hand on his arm. It was good to be able to touch him. She managed a smile. "You wanted to slow down."

"Yeah, but you've come to a grinding halt." His frown grew, gathering a whiff of temper. "You want to tell me what's up?"

No, she absolutely did not want to do that. So she kissed him again, hunting for the feelings, wanting to make him stop looking at her that way—but it went wrong. The fit wasn't there, the feelings didn't come rushing back in. Desperate to find it, she kissed him harder, reaching for him with both hands—

And knocked him in the head with her cast. She jerked her arm away, mortified—and he rolled off of her, cursing. And lay there, his chest heaving, one foot and thousands of miles away.

She sniffed. *Wrong, wrong, wrong,* the little voice inside her head chanted. *You've done it wrong again...*

At last he spoke. "Just what were you trying to prove?"

"Nothing." She sniffed. "I'm an idiot, but I don't have to prove that. The evidence is—" sniff "—already overwhelming."

His voice was strained. "Maggie, I'm trying to understand. You said you weren't trying to pay me back for hurting you last time, and I believe you, but—"

"Dammit," she muttered. Then said it again, louder. "Dammit!"

A pause. "You cursed."

"This seems to call for it." Curling up in a little ball and staying that way for the next year sounded like a good plan. She tucked her knees up to her chest and held on to them, her stupid, horrible cast very much in the way. If only he would just leave now...

The bed gave as he rolled over, moving closer. "You want to tell me what I'm supposed to think? First you set the stage for seduction, then you tell me to leave. Then you change your mind—and I'll admit I encouraged that. I thought I could stop things before they went too far, but—"

"For my own good," she said sarcastically.

"So shoot me. I meant well, but I've never indulged in noble sacrifices. Looks like I'm not any better at that than I am at drinking. Anyway, once we're in bed, you're with me one hundred percent. Then suddenly—you're gone. You kissed me as if your life depended on it, but, dammit, I can tell when a woman is turned off. So what happened?"

She sighed deeply. "Nothing that hasn't happened before."

"You mean this happened last time?" He laid a hand on her shoulder. "Maggie. I didn't—God in heaven. Tell me that last time I didn't keep going after you wanted to stop."

"You didn't keep going."

Silence. "At all?"

"You fell asleep."

His laughter came, soft and surprised. "If you weren't furious, you deserved to be. I passed out on you?"

"I guess." Actually, all this time she'd thought he'd just lost interest and dozed off. It made her feel better to think he'd passed out.

"Will you hate me if I say I'm glad?"

She scowled at her knees. "I might."

"Maggie." His voice was low and intense. "For the past year, I thought I'd been to bed with you and couldn't remember it. I'm glad there's nothing to remember. It means I didn't lose as much as I'd thought."

Slowly, reluctantly, she uncurled and sat up, careful not to look at him. "Now that we've got everything straightened out, do you think you could leave and let me die of humiliation in peace?"

"I don't think we've got much of anything straightened out." He propped himself up on one elbow, and in spite of herself, her eyes were drawn to him. He looked large and confident and utterly male stretched out on her bed. "Why, Maggie?" he asked softly.

She made a disgusted sound. "Stupid question. Women want to go to bed with you all the time."

He shook his head slowly. "You planned this. You don't think I have a right to know why you intended to seduce me?"

"No."

He was silent a moment. "You haven't forgiven me."

"That's not it! It—I—oh, I hate to fail." She scrambled off the bed. "I hate it, hate it, hate it." She headed for the pizza box, needing something to do. But when she lifted the lid, she saw cold pizza, the cheese congealed, grease staining the carton. She stared at it, wondering if she'd be able to choke any down.

"So how did you fail?" Luke's voice came from right behind her.

He wasn't going to go away, wasn't going to stop pushing for answers. Her shoulders slumped in defeat—and, maybe, a hint of relief. She let the lid of the box fall. "Do you remember why I was so bummed out when we met in Phoenix?"

"You'd been dumped by that idiot you'd been seeing." He squeezed her shoulder. "His mistake, you know. Hey—you're not carrying a torch for him, are you?"

"For Carl? Ha! Not likely. No, it's the reason he dumped me that—that bothers me. He did have a pretty good reason." She shrugged, trying to make it sound unimportant. "I guess I'm frigid."

Laughter was *not* the response she'd expected. Or wanted. She spun around and punched him. Hard. Right in his washboard abs.

He didn't have the courtesy to grunt, but he did rub his middle. "Ouch. Maggie, you didn't believe whatever nonsense Carl the jerk fed you, did you? You're about as far from frigid as jalapeños are from Häagen Dazs."

"If he'd been the only one…it happens every time, though. I like men," she said miserably. "I really do. And kissing, and all the rest of it. But every time…I get so far, and just when everything is feeling really good, it stops. Something inside me shuts down."

He didn't laugh that time. He put his arms around her and pulled her to him. "So," he said, resting his chin on top of her head. "What was I supposed to be—your cure? Uh-oh." He moved his head, trying to see her face. "You're not crying, are you?"

"Of course not." She sniffed and turned her head firmly away from his searching eyes. "I never cry. I can't. I—I'm no good at *any* of the woman things."

"Hmm. I guess that means you can't knit or make little doilies, either."

Her mouth twitched. "Or cook."

"Thank God for Sarita, then. Just as a matter of curiosity, when you said it happens every time—how many times are we talking about? Because I had the impression there hadn't been a huge number of men in your life."

She sniffed and tried to chuckle at the same time and nearly choked. "Luke, are you by any chance asking me how many men I've been to bed with?"

"Purely in an advisory capacity," he assured her, his hands stroking soothingly up her back.

"Well, I'm not telling you in any capacity. But you're right," she added with a sigh. "There haven't been that many. Enough, though, for me to know the problem isn't them. It's me."

"I see. Well, the first thing to do—" He scooped her up in his arms.

She squawked and grabbed his neck one-handed. "What are you doing?"

"The first step is to define the problem," he continued as if she hadn't spoken. He carried her to the room's only chair and sat down with her in his lap. "And you know, Maggie, I don't think your problem is sex."

In her current position, she couldn't help noticing that he hadn't lost interest in what they'd been doing before she humiliated herself. Not at all. "You know, Luke, I think you're a few bubbles shy of a bath. Of course the problem is sex."

"No, you don't seem to have any trouble there." He smiled at her as easily as if he weren't stone-hard and throbbing beneath her bottom. "You say you have a healthy interest in the opposite sex. You like kissing and—to use your words—all the rest of it, and my personal experience confirms that. Your problem isn't sex. It's climaxing."

She buried her flaming face against his shoulder.

"Have you ever climaxed?"

"I am *so* not going to answer that," she told his shirt.

"You also have a little trouble with communication. If you had discussed this with, ah, any of your other partners—"

"Oh, no. I tried that with Carl. Big mistake."

"You are talking about Carl Bronski, the baseball hunk with a room temperature IQ?"

She grinned without moving her face from its hiding place. "That's him. Carl might not be the sharpest knife in the drawer, but he's a really sweet guy. At least, he was until…"

"Until you crushed his ego with the news that you weren't seeing stars and rockets."

She sighed. "Yeah." His shirt was a soft, faded cotton. It felt good against her cheek. "I guess Carl wasn't a good choice for an intimate tête-à-tête."

"Especially if you used big words like that and confused him." His hand settled on her hip. "I can't help wondering…why me? I mean, after the fiasco last year…though I didn't know until tonight just how much of a disaster that was, you did. Why would you want to, ah…"

For once he was having trouble getting the words out. She liked that. "Seduce you? A lot of reasons." Some of which she had no intention of revealing—like the fact that she used to be in love with him. "For one thing, if things didn't go well, I didn't think you'd get all bent out of shape about it. You *know* you're good."

He was silent a moment. "Excuse me. Did you accidentally compliment me just now?"

She grinned and, at last, felt comfortable enough to straighten, which put her head even with his. Her fingers had made a mess of his hair, she noticed. Good. At least some part of him was ruffled—*every* part of her was. "You can take it that way if you like," she said generously.

An odd shadow passed through his eyes. "So that's why you picked me? Because you thought I wouldn't make you feel even worse about yourself?"

"Well, your ego wouldn't be involved, so—Luke? Is something wrong?"

"Other than the obvious, you mean?" He smiled wryly and shifted his legs, settling her more on his thighs, less on that interesting bulge. "No. Go on. Tell me more about what a great lover you thought I'd make."

"I don't think so. You've heard too much of that already." He'd heard too much of all sorts of things tonight. Right this moment she felt more relieved than embarrassed about it, but Maggie knew herself too well to believe that would last. By tomorrow morning she'd be hunting for ways to live with Luke without ever having to face him again.

Just thinking about tomorrow brought the first lick of mortification to her cheeks. "Uh...I think it's time for me to crawl off and lick my wounds in private now." Rather awkwardly she slid off his lap.

"All right. Order something from room service," he said, standing and starting for the door. "I don't think that pizza is going to get eaten tonight."

"Probably not." He'd agreed to leave easily enough now that he knew all her secrets. And why not? In spite of his lingering arousal, he wouldn't want to hang around and try again after all she'd told him. And could she blame him? She wasn't sure she'd want to try again, anyway. She'd be so horribly self-conscious she'd be bound to fail.

No, she thought, trailing after him unhappily. Best to put tonight and her stupid plan behind her, forget any of it had ever happened.

Luke opened the door but paused, turning to look at her. He didn't say anything. Just stood there studying her face, which was rapidly growing hotter.

"What is it?" she said crossly. "Did you forget something?"

He shook his head. His mouth smiled, but his eyes were sad. "A last word of advice. Sex isn't a competition, Maggie. It isn't something you can fail at—or win." More briskly, he added, "Now, don't bother coming up with ways to avoid me. I'm not going to let you hide away and convince yourself you're humiliated.''

''You know me too well.''

''Besides,'' he said, tracing a finger along her cheek, ''I still have to seduce you.''

''Wh-what?''

His smile widened slowly, packing tons of wicked suggestions in one subtle curve. ''You don't need to be the seducer, Maggie. You need to be seduced. The best way to stop trying to win is to lose right off the bat. Lose control. Lose...'' His finger did delicious and scary things along the line of her parted lips. ''Everything.''

When the door closed gently behind him, Maggie was still standing stock-still, her lips tingling.

At midnight, Luke was still awake. He sat in the darkness with the TV turned on and the sound turned off, his legs stretched in front of him, slouching low in the uncomfortable chair his hotel room boasted. He'd pulled the drapes back so he could look out the window at the city lights spangling in the darkness twenty floors below.

The room had other amenities that made up for the uncomfortable chair. He was sipping at one of them, a neat glass of Scotch he'd poured from the second tiny bottle he'd opened after leaving Maggie alone in her room.

He should have stayed with her. He'd meant to. He'd cuddled her in his lap with that in mind, planning to get her used to his physical nearness. He'd intended to stay the night with her, to sleep with her—chastely, at first. Women needed holding. It was a truth that was so obvious to Luke he didn't understand why more men couldn't see it. Some women longed for arms around them more than they hungered after the fireworks Maggie was worried about, and accepted sex as the price of being held.

And why not? he thought moodily. Hadn't he taken the same sort of comfort himself at times?

In the morning, he could have finished taking care of Maggie. When she was all drowsy, her defenses down, unable to think about what she was supposed to do or feel, he could have stroked her gently to climax. Once she'd been taken to that place of sweet, sensual oblivion, she'd have no trouble finding her way back. All she really needed was to believe in herself.

Oh, yeah. He'd known just how to handle Maggie. Wasn't that why she'd come to him? Because he knew so very much about pleasing women. He grimaced and sipped the cheap Scotch, gazing out the window at the neon-streaked city night. The problem was, he didn't know how to handle himself. Not with Maggie. Not anymore.

When had he fallen in love with her?

He couldn't pinpoint a time, a moment. Looking back, it seemed as if he'd been headed that way for years without noticing. He knew exactly when he'd realized it, though. He'd been holding her on his lap, her crimson face hidden against his shoulder as she explained that she'd wanted to go to bed with him because it wouldn't hurt his ego if she "failed" again.

She was right about one thing. It wasn't his ego that hurt.

He smiled bitterly and toasted the darkness. He was in love with Maggie, and she wanted to use him for a little friendly sex. The irony of it was hard to miss. Or the justice.

The question was—what was he going to do about it?

Nine

The hotel had a pleasant little green-and-white restaurant on the second floor with a breakfast buffet. That's where Luke dragged Maggie the next morning.

She'd slept very little. As a result, she'd heard Luke leave the room next to hers shortly after midnight. He'd been gone for hours. Or possibly all night—she couldn't be sure, since she had eventually fallen into a miserable, exhausted slumber. No fuzzy memories for her when she woke up, either. Every detail of the previous night's events had been painfully clear in her mind the second her eyes had opened. Her goal had been equally clear: get out of the hotel and back to the ranch without seeing Luke.

Luke knew her too well. He'd been at her door by seven-thirty, and had alternately teased her and bullied her until she found herself showered, dressed and sitting down across from him.

Luke eyed her heavily loaded plate. "Speaking as your trainer—"

"I missed supper last night," she pointed out and flushed, wishing she hadn't referred to any part of the night before.

This was one heck of a morning after, wasn't it?

"Speaking as your trainer," he said again, scooping up a forkful of his own eggs, "that's a good way to start the day. Plenty of protein and fresh fruit."

"Oh." Having successfully defended her right to an appetite, she stirred her eggs around indifferently. Maybe the ham would taste okay, she thought, and cut a piece. And looked at it, trying to drum up some interest in chewing and swallowing.

"Before we check out, I need you to help me smuggle a cat out of my room."

"A cat." She put her fork down. "You have a cat in your room?"

He nodded and took a bite of bacon. "Ornery beast, too. It took me two hours to coax her out from under the bushes last night."

"You were out coaxing a cat last night?" *A cat—not a woman.* Relief hit, making her giddy. She covered the reaction by taking a hasty sip of coffee.

Last night while staring up at the ceiling, Maggie had told herself over and over that Luke wouldn't have gone looking for a woman to have sex with. He'd promised her fidelity. But at two in the morning, that had seemed like a flimsy reed to grasp. Especially since she knew what kind of condition he'd been in when he left her room.

Especially since she knew Luke hadn't been faithful to his first wife.

"Jacob called and asked me to get the cat."

"Jacob wanted you to coax a cat. After midnight." She grinned, her appetite suddenly back full-force, and popped the ham in her mouth. Delicious. "Sounds like quite a story. Tell me about it."

He did, while she finished her breakfast, though he was lamentably short of details. Jacob had called Luke from the hospital. From what Maggie could piece together, one of Jacob's employees had suffered a break-in at her house. The woman's cousin had been badly beaten, and in the confusion, her cat had gotten out. Jacob had asked Luke to find the animal since, for some reason, he was determined that the woman not go back to her house.

Maggie pushed her empty plate away and leaned back, satisfyingly full. "So this woman—the one whose cat you rescued—is Jacob's new assistant?"

"Yeah." Luke had already finished and was on his third cup of coffee.

"What happened to Sonia?"

"She's on leave. Her daughter just made her a grandma, so Jacob had to get someone in temporarily. There was something in his voice when he spoke about his new assistant…" He grinned. "I'm looking forward to meeting Claire McGuire."

"You think he's interested in her?"

He nodded and caught the eye of a hovering waiter, indicating he was ready for the check. He signed it and stood. "Does that bother you?"

Surprised, she stood, too. "No, why would it?"

He gave her a wry look. "He did ask you to marry him."

"Oh, that." She searched his face, wondering—hoping—he might be a tiny bit jealous. "He had to ask someone, because of Ada and the trust. I was handy."

He snorted. "This city is full of women who would love to be handy to Jacob in that way."

"Well—he does likes me, I think. And I guess he trusted me. Jacob doesn't trust a lot of people."

"True." He slung a friendly arm around her shoulder. "Come on. Let's go smuggle a cat."

Maggie wasn't sure how she wound up with Luke. She had her truck now; she'd intended to leave for the ranch once they finished their cat-smuggling, but somehow she ended up in his pickup. First they had to buy a cat carrier. Then they had to take the cat to its owner.

Luke seemed to think she really was nervous about driving on the highway by herself, and she couldn't very well tell him she'd made that up because she'd needed an excuse to stay in the city and seduce him.

They pulled up in front of the West mansion a little after ten. Maggie had only been there twice—once with Luke and some mutual friends several years ago, and once with Jacob.

It was, to say the least, unusual.

Luke's grandfather had built the house back when the area had been more rural than urban. It was a high, stone-walled transplant from another age, with a crenelated roof, gargoyles, a magnificent garden and an honest-to-God turret. Today, Christmas lights strung against the gray stone lent it an incongruously cheerful note. She smiled as she hopped down from the pickup. "I love this house. It would be perfect if only you had a ghost."

Luke gave her an amused look. "I seem to remember you complaining about our lack of a family haunt before."

She nodded, pleased that he'd remembered. Since most of his attention on her prior visit with him had been taken up by the blonde he'd been dating at the time, she was also surprised.

He took her hand. Her heart did a quick, foolish jig.

He gave her a quizzical glance. "Your palm is damp. Are you nervous about seeing Jacob again?"

She grimaced. "Stupid, isn't it? It isn't as if I broke his heart or anything. But this feels weird."

"Hmm. I can see how it might. You and he dated for a couple of months. Now here you are—married to me." He gave her hand a last squeeze and reached back in the pickup for the cat carrier, where a huge, unhappy calico was making her opinion known.

In truth, Maggie's nerves had less to do with seeing Jacob again than with the way Luke had been holding her hand—firmly. Almost possessively, making her foolish heart entertain all sorts of silly ideas. Maybe he *was* jealous. At least a little bit.

Of course, there wasn't much for him to be jealous of. Occasionally Jacob needed a date for a business-type party, and she'd been happy to oblige. Being seen on Jacob West's arm was a boost in the ego for any woman. Other than that, they hadn't dated seriously—a play, a couple of movies, a couple of dinners. Their relationship had never gone beyond friendly. She'd enjoyed his company, especially since he hadn't pressured her for sex the way some men did.

And seeing him had been a connection of sorts with Luke...

"So," Luke said, swinging the cat carrier over the side of the truck. "Did you go to bed with him?"

She sucked in a breath so suddenly that she choked and started coughing. "I don't—I—why in the world did you ask me that?"

"I thought I'd try Sarita's approach—if you want to

know, ask. Never mind. It's none of my business." He held out his keys. "You get the door while I lug this monster up to the porch."

"No," she blurted.

He paused, hand still extended "No, you won't get the door?"

"No, we, uh, didn't. You know." She couldn't tell a thing from his expression. It was as closed as his brother's so often was.

Finally his eyebrows lifted. "You dated Jacob for over two months and never made it into his bed?"

"I wasn't *aiming* for his bed."

"Come on, Maggie. I know my brother. Women may not line up next to his bed every night, but he's never had to look hard to find one ready to trip and fall into it, either."

"Oh, well—I guess I was lying, then. Either that or I've got a terrible memory. Let's see, did I go to bed with Jacob, or not?" She tapped her finger on her chin and hummed a few bars of the *Jeopardy* music. "Gee, maybe I did and it slipped my mind. With all the hundreds of men I've been with, it's easy to lose track."

He laughed. "All right, all right. I shouldn't have doubted you. Here." He gave her the keys and started for the front door. "I hope you're ready to be cross-examined."

He was whistling, cheerful. Was he relieved that she'd never been intimate with his brother? *Give it up,* she told herself sternly. Luke was as incapable of jealousy as he was of—of other emotions. And that was a good thing, under the circumstances. Wasn't it?

"I don't think Jacob will cross-examine us," she said as she came up beside him at the door.

''Not Jacob. Ada. I e-mailed Jacob about our little trip to Las Vegas, and I imagine he told Ada.''

''Luke.'' She stared at him. ''You *e-mailed* your brother the news of our marriage?''

''Sure. I didn't want him to find out from the lawyers. They were likely to contact him sooner or later, once I'd sent them our marriage license.'' He patted her shoulder with his free hand. ''Don't worry. I'll rescue you from Ada as soon as possible.''

Ada commandeered Maggie the minute they stepped in the door. She would have dragged Luke off to her lair in the kitchen, too, but he had to deliver the cat. Or so he pointed out.

He would rather have carried Maggie off to his own lair, upstairs. He wanted her with a dull ache that had nearly exploded the moment he knew she'd never been with his brother. He wanted to celebrate, to claim her—and maybe he wouldn't have minded putting off the confrontation he was headed for now.

Luke had known all along he had no right to be jealous. The whole time Jacob had been dating Maggie, he'd known that—and it had eaten at him anyway. Luke wasn't used to jealousy. He hadn't had a clue how to deal with it. He'd avoided his brother—hell, he'd avoided everyone, holing up at the ranch and working himself into exhaustion. He hadn't wanted to hear some friendly acquaintance pair Maggie's name with his brother's. And still the acid had eaten at him.

There was a huge difference between having no right to jealousy and having no reason for it.

He was whistling the theme to *Star Wars* as he headed down the hall to his brother's office. He'd taken the first hurdle, and it had gone better than he'd had any reason to hope. There was another tough one coming up.

One quick knock on Jacob's door. Then he pushed it open.

Maggie sat at the big, square table in a kitchen that smelled deliciously of cinnamon and yeast and watched the woman Luke loved. Ada was pouring them both a cup of coffee.

She hadn't offered Maggie any of the coffee cake that was cooling on the counter.

The little housekeeper made Maggie think of a dandelion—tough and scrawny. Her hair was an unlikely yellow, and it frizzed around her leathery face like a dandelion puff. She wore faded jeans, a purple sweatshirt that warned, I'm Out Of Estrogen, And I've Got A Gun, and diamond earrings. The stones were big enough to blind a person if the light caught them right.

It was hard to imagine anyone less like the very proper Marilyn who opened doors and waxed floors at her parents' house than this woman. Maggie smiled. "I like your sweatshirt."

"Me, too." Ada set the mugs down and took a seat. Her eyes were as sharp as her words. "Why did you marry Luke after stringing Jacob along?"

"I didn't!" she sputtered. "String Jacob along, I mean. He didn't really want to marry me."

"Then why did he ask you?"

Tricky question. Maggie picked her mug up in both hands and sipped to give herself time to think. Luke had warned her several days ago that Ada didn't know what he and his brothers were doing for her. Privately Maggie thought that was foolish. Ada was bound to find it odd when they all got married, bam-bam-bam. But she wouldn't be the one to spill the beans. "I guess he thought it was time to marry. You know Jacob. He plans everything out logically."

Ada nodded slowly. "I can see him doing something like that. But how did you jump from one brother to the other so quick?"

"It wasn't that quick. I mean it was, but...Jacob and I were just friends. And Luke..." Inspiration struck. "We were involved last year, but it didn't work out." True. Misleading, but true. "When Luke heard I'd turned Jacob down, he realized, ah, how he felt and asked me to marry him." It sounded so good she almost believed it herself.

"Does that mean you were in love with Luke while you were seeing Jacob?"

Maggie flushed. "That makes me sound like either a slut or an idiot."

"So which are you?"

"An idiot," she said promptly. "I must be, or I wouldn't answer your nosy questions."

Ada gave a single, loud hoot of laughter. She stood and patted Maggie on the shoulder. "I'll get you a piece of coffee cake."

The cat had been released into the rooms that adjoined Jacob's office, which had been converted to a combination office/living area for Sonia, and were currently occupied by Claire McGuire. Jacob's assistant was still asleep after a long night at the hospital; her cousin was out of danger, but, from what Jacob had said, she wasn't.

Luke moved restlessly around the room. Jacob stood beside his desk, scowling. "I suppose I should wish you luck. I'd rather knock you across the room."

Last week, Luke would have jumped at the chance to

punch his brother out—or try to. Not now. "You can pound on me if it will make you feel better."

"Maggie is a special woman."

"I agree." He studied Jacob's face. "You don't think I'll be good for her."

"Do you?"

Luke gave a short, hard laugh and scrubbed a hand over his hair. "Hell, no."

"If you cheat on her, I'll pound you into the ground."

"I promised her fidelity. You think I'm going to break that promise?"

That his brother hesitated before answering hurt more than Luke would have thought. "No," Jacob said at last. "You don't break your promises. I think you feel something for her, but damned if I know what that is."

Luke wasn't about to tell him the truth, so he grinned. "What, you think I'm going to give you an excuse to pound me?"

"Dammit, if all you want is some playtime in bed—"

"I wouldn't have had to marry her for that." Which came closer to the truth than he liked, so he switched the subject. "Now, what about you? I've done my bit, and I understand Michael is ready to do his when he gets back. He said you've got your eye on another candidate for Mrs. Jacob West."

Jacob picked up his pen and played with it. A delaying tactic? Luke wondered. How interesting.

"You talked to Michael?"

"He called me before he went off to play in whatever corner of the world he could find people willing to shoot at him."

Jacob's mouth crooked up. "It could be worse. If he'd

stayed on his original career path, he'd be getting shot at by people in this country. With badges.''

"Yeah. And maybe some without badges.''

The door to his assistant's office swung open, and a spectacularly beautiful woman hurried in. She was wearing an elegant little suit, and every one of her bright red hairs were in place. Her makeup was understated, flawless. And she was barefoot.

"Jacob, I need to talk—oh.'' She stopped dead when she saw Luke. "Excuse me. I didn't realize you had someone with you.''

Jacob's smile was a revelation—proprietary. Tender. "Claire, I don't think you've met my brother Luke. Luke, this is Claire McGuire.''

"It's a pleasure to meet you, Claire.'' Luke's gaze slid over her, and his smile widened. "Very much my pleasure. Tell me you aren't involved with my stuffy big brother.''

Jacob slipped an arm around her waist and pulled her up against his side. "I asked Claire to marry me last night.''

And just that easily, the second hurdle was behind him, and it had been an easy jump, after all. He hadn't wrecked his relationship with his brother by marrying Maggie. The look in Jacob's eyes told him that. Luke grinned, delighted. "Did you, now? You've always had good taste. Claire, come here and let me welcome you to the family properly.''

"I'm afraid you're premature,'' Claire said dryly "So is Jacob. I haven't accepted.''

"No, Michael was premature. I was two weeks late, which my mother never let me forget. Jacob, of course, was right on time. Except this once?'' He raised one eyebrow. "Did you rush your fences, Jacob?''

"We're negotiating."

"Negotiating?" Luke laughed. "First time I've heard it called that."

Jacob scowled. "It's time someone taught you some manners."

Claire—obviously a sensible woman—ignored him. "You're the magician who found my cat and coaxed her into coming with you, aren't you? I want to thank you for that. You don't seem to be bleeding anywhere."

"She was reluctant, but a lot of females are wary of strange men. Fortunately I discovered her weakness for ham."

"I suspect you're good at that sort of thing—coaxing wary females. Almost as good as you are at getting a rise out of your brother."

"I usually have to work a lot harder than this to ruffle Jacob's feathers. Maybe he's short on sleep this morning."

She grinned. "He is."

Aha. Luke's grin widened. When his brother placed a hard, proprietary kiss on his assistant's mouth, Luke figured he'd learned everything he needed to know. "Guess I'd better be going," he said cheerfully.

"Oh—wait," Claire said. "Don't hurry off on my account."

"Luke was about to leave anyway," Jacob said. "I think we've said everything we needed to." He met Luke's eyes, his arm still around Claire's waist.

Luke nodded. "Yeah, I think we have. I need to rescue Maggie, anyway. Ada has her pinned in the kitchen. I'm looking forward to seeing more of you, Claire. Not as much of you as Jacob does, of course—"

"Luke." Jacob made the name a warning.

Unrepentant, Luke tossed them a last grin and a wave and headed for the door.

Ten

The creak of leather. The warmth beneath her. The smell of horse, and the vast blue arch overhead. The weather had continued sunny and mild all weekend, with just enough of a breeze to lift the hair around her face.

Maggie sighed happily. Even at a walk, there was nothing she liked better than taking Fine Dandy out.

"So why'd you give your horse such a dorky name?"

She smiled at the boy riding beside her. Jeremy made her think of a sepia-toned Huck Finn. He had the tousled hair, the attitude, even the freckles—a sprinkling of darker brown on honey-colored skin. Most of the time he lacked Huck's grin, but when it appeared the resemblance was complete. His eyes were sharp, green and often suspicious. On the ground, he was all knees and elbows. On horseback he was at home.

She knew the feeling. "His name was registered before

I got him, but it suits him. He is a bit of a dandy. Just look at him. Thinks he's pretty special, doesn't he?''

"Yeah." Jeremy eyed the way Dandy walked, the proud arch of his neck holding his head high. "He thinks he's hot stuff, all right. But he's, like, a mongrel, isn't he? Not a pure anything."

Maggie's heart twisted. How often had Jeremy been made to feel he wasn't a "pure anything"? "That's one way to put it. Dandy inherited the best of both worlds—the speed of a Thoroughbred, the strength and patience of a warmblood."

"But he'd be worth more if he was a Thoroughbred." The shuttered look on Jeremy's face challenged her to prove him wrong. "Not some mixed-up breed."

"Actually, no. When he was young and untried that might have been true, but now that he's proven himself at events, he's worth a great deal of money."

"Yeah? So how come we never hear about horses like him? Everyone thinks Thoroughbreds are the best."

"Thoroughbreds get all the good press," Maggie agreed. "And they're wonderful for racing. Jumping, too. Some people do use them for eventing because of their speed, but they have problems with dressage—too temperamental. And they often lack the endurance for cross-country. Three-day eventing is grueling." She patted Dandy's neck. "You need a horse with everything—speed, manners, endurance and guts. A winner's heart."

Jeremy didn't say anything more, leaving Maggie to wonder if she was doing this all wrong. Had she made it too obvious she wasn't just talking about horses? She sighed. What did she know about handling a troubled child? One who, according to Luke, didn't think of himself as a child.

She did see the child in Jeremy at times, but, like his grin, it appeared all too seldom.

The Sunday afternoon ride seemed to be a tradition when Jeremy stayed at the ranch—which, apparently, happened every weekend Luke wasn't at a show or an event. The ride was Jeremy's reward for making an effort to follow the rules all weekend. He had managed that, though not without complaint. Except when it came to riding. There, Luke bore down hard on the boy. And there, Jeremy accepted the demands, seemed to thrive under them. Whether consciously or not, he responded to the assumption behind the discipline: that he was capable of excellence, and neither he nor Luke were interested in less than his best.

But early that afternoon one of Luke's mares had developed colic. A disorder that made babies cranky and miserable could, in extreme cases, kill a horse. Luke hadn't wanted to leave the mare until he was sure she was going to be all right, so Maggie had volunteered to take Jeremy riding across the ranch's rolling acres.

At first he'd been sullen. The boy obviously worshiped Luke, for all that he tried to hide it behind a major dose of attitude. He talked street-smart and tough—and all weekend, wherever Luke was, Jeremy was somewhere nearby, a skinny shadow.

Jeremy had been especially disgusted about changing his riding partner because they couldn't gallop. A sedate canter was the best Maggie should attempt with her wrist. And then Luke had ordered Jeremy to stay with her.

"Oh, like I can't handle a horse on my own," Jeremy had said with that sneer he was so fond of. "Or maybe you think I'd steal it."

"No, like you're going riding with a lady whose wrist

is in a cast," Luke had replied calmly. "What if Maggie has trouble and you aren't around?"

Jeremy had darted her a suspicious glance. "I thought she was supposed to be a hotshot rider."

"If you work really hard, you might be as good as Maggie in another ten years. But I've told you often enough that even a good rider on a good horse can get in trouble. And she does have a broken wrist." He'd given Maggie a stern look. "Frankly, if I thought she'd pay any attention, I'd forbid her to go out without me. As it is, I'll have to delegate my responsibilities to you."

Jeremy's face had perked up—either because he liked the idea of being delegated adult responsibilities, or because he was interested in anyone who flouted authority. "She don't listen to you, huh?"

Luke had shaken his head sadly. "Hardly ever."

"You ought to listen to Luke," Jeremy had told Maggie seriously. "He knows everything about riding and horses."

"I do, when he's speaking as my trainer."

"Just not when he's bein' your husband? Why not?"

Why not, indeed? Maggie thought now. Maybe because she wasn't really his wife, any more than he was really her husband. Although he'd acted like a husband all weekend...when they were around Jeremy.

Blast the man. He kept *touching* her. All weekend, he'd found excuses to put an arm around her waist, play with her hair or plant a quick kiss. Unconsciously Maggie's hands tightened on the reins, making Dandy sidle.

"I guess he wishes he could gallop, too," Jeremy said.

"Probably. But just now he was reacting to my hands. I gave him mixed signals."

"I didn't see you do anything."

For the next few minutes she talked to Jeremy about

the signals a well-trained horse responded to. He knew
some of it, of course, from his lessons, but he was like
a sponge where horses were concerned, eager to soak up
everything he could.

It was an easier subject than the one that preyed on
her mind.

Luke claimed he wanted Jeremy to see them as a couple. He said the boy needed to see healthy male-female
relationships. How could she argue with that? *But he
doesn't have to touch me all the time to do it,* she thought
aggrievedly.

They were nearly to the house when Jeremy spoke
again. "I figured that business about looking out for you
was a bunch of crap. You didn't need me."

"Oh, I think Luke's plan worked pretty well."

"Kept me from having a good run, you mean?" He
lifted one corner of his lip in that sneer.

Maybe she should try telling him what her grandmother had once told her—if he weren't careful, his face
would freeze that way. "No, it kept *me* from having a
good run. I would have been tempted to if you weren't
along. As it was, I had to set a good example."

That startled a grin out of him. "He was conning
you?"

In another few years, she thought, the girls were going
to be in trouble. That grin lit his face up like the star on
a Christmas tree. She nodded. "Did a good job of it, too,
didn't he?"

"He tricked us both, didn't he? I couldn't gallop because of you, and you couldn't gallop because of me."

They'd reached the stable. She swung down from
Dandy's back and pulled the reins over his head. "Maybe
we should trick him back."

"What, like have a race and not tell him?" Jeremy turned suspicious eyes on her.

Maggie was vastly pleased with his disapproval. The boy wanted the adults around him to know right from wrong—and choose to do right. It said a lot about him. She started into the stable, leading her horse. "I was thinking more about Christmas trees. Luke doesn't want one. I do."

He followed with Samson. "So?"

"So you're coming here next weekend, right? I thought you and I might go buy a tree. If you're part of the deal," she said, stopping at Dandy's stall, "Luke won't fuss as much."

"Oh, sure. Like that matters to him."

"You are a kid, you know. Adults have a hard time refusing kids that sort of thing this time of year. Besides..." She slipped Dandy's bridle off. "He likes you a lot."

He shrugged one skinny shoulder and tried to look indifferent. "I guess I could go with you."

"We'll have to pick out all the decorations, too," she warned him.

"If you want to." He was trying so hard to act as if he didn't care one way or another, but Maggie caught the gleam of excitement in his eyes. "I don't know if I'll be much good at it. I've never picked out Christmas stuff. Not a whole tree's worth, anyway." He turned to his horse, loosening the girth. "My mom used to let me pick out one ornament, though. Every year. It was kind of a tradition."

Maggie felt that squeezing in her chest again. Jeremy never referred to his mother. It's a good thing, she thought, that she never cried, or she might embarrass them both. "I've never picked out decorations for an en-

tire tree, either. But what's to be good at? We'll just get
what we like.'' She prayed she was doing the right thing.
If Luke's dislike for Christmas stemmed from his long-
ago loss, maybe it would help him to focus on the needs
of another child. One who mattered.

And Jeremy was going to have a ball picking out ''a
whole tree's worth'' of decorations. She'd see to that.
She sniffed and said cheerfully, ''Hey, could you help
me with this saddle? I can't get it off one-handed.''

Jeremy looked out the window and watched another
highway marker whiz by. Going back was always a pain.
The only good part was that the drive took over an hour,
and Jeremy got to spend the time with Luke. He'd wondered if this time Luke's new wife would come along,
and had been relieved when she didn't.

Less than an hour now, he thought. In less than an
hour he'd be back at the Pearsons's. Then there would
be five endless days of school and homework before
he could come to the ranch again.

Assuming Luke wanted him to come back. So far, he
had. So far, every time he'd told Jeremy he would be
there to pick him up, he'd shown up just as he said he
would. Except this last Friday, and that hadn't been
Luke's fault. Mrs. Pearson had called him and told him
not to, on account of that stupid school project.

According to the law, Mr. and Mrs. Pearson were in
charge of him. The law sucked. Jeremy didn't need anyone to be in charge of him. But if he had—well, if he
had, he wouldn't mind so much if it could have been
Luke.

Luke probably didn't want the hassle, though. Except
on weekends. He didn't seem to mind if Jeremy hung
around then.

"If you scowl any harder, you're going to crack the glass," Luke commented.

Jeremy looked at Luke and tried to lift one brow the way Luke did sometimes. "I guess you can afford to fix it if it breaks."

"I guess you can afford to spend another hour on chores every weekend if you do break it."

A grin slipped across his face before he could stop it. Every weekend. That sounded good. Really good. Maybe he really should break a window, just to make sure he'd be coming back.

"So what did you think of Maggie?" Luke asked.

"She's a fox," Jeremy said, more out of a desire to compliment his friend's taste than because he'd noticed her appearance much. More genuinely he added, "She's okay. She smiles a lot, but not like Mrs. Pearson."

"Oh? How does Mrs. Pearson smile?"

"Like she's got hemorrhoids and don't—*doesn't* want anyone to guess."

Luke's laugh opened that warm, funny place inside Jeremy. It felt good, yet it didn't. He squirmed in the seat. "So how come you married her, anyway? I mean, you're not doin' her—"

"Real men don't talk about 'doing' women," Luke said. "It's rude. It sounds like a kid bragging about scoring a touchdown."

The guys he hung with wouldn't agree, but the guys he hung with weren't real men, like Luke was. More like wannabes. "You're not sleeping with her." He paused, waiting to see if that phrasing was okay. When Luke didn't comment, he went on. "So I guess you didn't knock her up or anything. And you're not, like, goofy on her, or you'd be sleeping with her."

"I am not going to discuss my relationship with Maggie."

Jeremy knew that tone of voice, knew he ought to let it go. But he couldn't. It mattered too much. "I just wondered. I mean, one day you're not even dating her, and the next—bam. You married her."

Luke didn't say anything at first. Whenever he was silent that way, it made Jeremy twitchy, as if his arms and legs needed to be doing something. Anything. Lots of things, all at once. He couldn't stand it if Luke was mad at him, but he had to *know*.

Once he'd asked Ms. Hammond, his social worker, if single guys ever adopted kids. He'd made out like he wasn't talking about himself, but she'd given him one of those looks, the kind that saw right inside him. Ms. Hammond was okay, though. She hadn't made a big deal about it. She'd just said that it was really hard for a single man to adopt a child. The courts wanted kids to go to a home with a married couple.

Another reason the law sucked, in Jeremy's opinion. What was the big deal about being married? It didn't make people nicer. It sure didn't make them willing to put up with a "troubled youngster." Jeremy knew that's what they called him—troubled. He knew what it meant, too. He came from trouble. He *was* trouble.

"Maggie and I got married because we wanted to be together," Luke said at last. "There were other reasons, but they aren't any of your business."

Jeremy shrugged to show he didn't care, but deep inside, hope twisted, hard and bright and painful, as hard to ignore as a loose tooth. He had to poke at the feeling, wiggle it, see how it fit.

Maybe—just maybe—those "other reasons" involved him. Maybe Luke had decided he didn't want to be single anymore, because single men couldn't adopt kids. Maybe...

Jeremy swallowed hard. It was stupid to think that maybe Luke wanted to be in charge of him all the time, not just on weekends. That he might have a real home one of these days. A home...and a dad.

The house was so empty. Maggie had only been here a week. It shouldn't feel so strange to be alone.

But she hadn't been alone all week, she reminded herself as she wandered into the big living room, carrying the glass of wine she was supposed to be relaxing with. It was the change that had her spirits sagging, that was all. All week, there had been others around. Sarita. Her husband and the other hands. Jeremy.

And Luke. She bit her lip. It was Luke's absence she was feeling. How silly. She would enjoy the privacy. In another minute or two, the house would stop feeling abandoned, and she would definitely enjoy having some time to herself.

She drifted over to the big window and stood there looking out, sipping at a mediocre Chardonnay. She smiled. Luke had excellent taste about a lot of things, but he clearly had no palate. She supposed he didn't drink enough to tell one wine from another.

He'd been drunk that night in Phoenix, though, drunk enough to blot out much of his memory of that night. It had been...oh, yes, she thought grimly. December 22. The anniversary of his baby's death.

She hadn't thought about that anniversary last year. Nine years was a long time, and she'd assumed Luke was over his grief. After all, the baby had never lived to be born. Although, at seven months, it had been old enough to have lived outside the womb, had it been given a chance...

It? Had the baby been a girl or a boy? She couldn't remember, and her failure shamed her. Easier to think of *it* than of him or her, wasn't it? Easier, but a cheat, a coward's trick for tucking the truth out of sight. The sort of thing her mother did so well—tidying away unpleasantness, pretending it didn't exist. Maggie wasn't happy to find herself doing it.

Pamela hadn't killed an *it* when she'd swallowed those sleeping pills. She'd killed her baby. Luke's baby.

Was death less of a loss if you'd never held your child in your arms? Or more?

"Hey, Maggie-may-I." The sound of the front door closing snapped her out of her thoughts. "Was there anything left in the refrigerator for supper? Jeremy tends to empty it out."

Just his voice. That's all it took to make her heart silly and for warmth to pool in her belly. Maggie didn't turn around. She didn't dare. "I hope you weren't counting on having the last of the roast for your supper, because I did. Oh, and your brother called. Jacob."

"I grabbed a hamburger on the way back. What did Jacob have to say?"

"He and Claire are getting married at the end of the month. He sounded—well, not lighthearted, exactly." She had to smile at using "lighthearted" and "Jacob West" in the same sentence. "But I have a feeling this marriage means more to him than getting the trust dissolved. You should call him back."

"I will. Later." He came up behind her. "Why are you standing here in the dark?"

"It isn't dark yet," she protested, but when she looked over her shoulder she saw that it was, here in the house.

Outside, the light was fading in the gradual way of winter, streaking the sky in quiet shades of rose and amethyst and ever-darkening blues.

Inside, the shadows had already thickened, drawing night to them. Maybe that was what made Luke look suddenly strange to her. His smile was as crooked and charming as ever. His clothes were no different than what he usually wore—cotton and denim, both softened by wear. But there was no color to his shirt now, and no reading his eyes in the gathering darkness.

It was imagination, surely, that painted his expression with some mysterious tension.

"You look all broody." There was nothing different about his voice—or the effect it had on her. "Is something wrong?"

"Just having a mood." She looked out the window again. The light was leaking away, while dusk seemed to rise up from the earth like a fog, covering trees, rocks and the pale, brittle grass of winter.

Why did the sight make her heart beat so fast, as if sending out an alarm? She shook her head, baffled by herself. "Most of the time I love evenings and winter. Except for the cold. I don't like being cold."

"Maybe I'm missing something. What else is there to winter but the cold?" He moved close behind her and put his hands on her hips.

His hands were warm. Very warm. So was his body, so close to hers but not—quite—touching. "Oh, there's a lot more to winter than cold weather. Short days and long nights, hot chocolate and fires in the fireplace. And snow. I love snow, even if it is cold. And there's the holidays, and…you need to move your hands."

"Okay." He did move them. Slowly. Up from her hips

to her waist to her sides, stopping with his fingers just below her breasts.

Her heart thudded hard. "I meant *remove* your hands."

"No." And he moved his hands again—to cover her breasts.

She gasped. "You can't just *do* that. I said—"

"Of course I can." He spread his fingers wide, lifting. Pressing firmly. His breath was warm on her nape when he nuzzled her there. "You're not in control here, Maggie. You'll let me put my hands on you, and my mouth."

"I..." It seemed that she would. A delicious languor was fuzzing her brain and loosening her muscles. His tongue traced the cord along the side of her neck, and there seemed no reason not to let her head fall back against his shoulder.

Still... "This is supposed to be my decision. Our decision, I mean. If we make love..." She briefly lost the point of her sentence when his thumbs slid lazily over her nipples. "It's supposed to be mutual."

"Maggie." His voice was rich and warm and amused. "You're too used to competing. You'd try to take charge, then you'd worry about getting it right. This time, you aren't the rider. You're the horse."

"That's a..." Her breath caught as his thumbs continued to stroke, making her want to arch her back like a cat. "A lousy line. Is that supposed to be seductive? Telling me I'm a horse?"

"You'll follow my signals." He caught her nipple between his thumbs and the sides of his hands, and squeezed lightly. "Won't you?"

She nearly choked on a laugh. Oh, this was crazy. How could she want to laugh and punch him and rip off his clothes, all at the same time?

"You smell so good." He pressed a kiss to her neck.

"Almost as good as you feel, all soft and hot and willing. I ache for you, Maggie." He pressed himself against her, and she knew it was true.

This, then, was the seduction he'd promised. Maggie tried to figure out what she should do, but she couldn't sort it all out, not when his hands made such distracting magic on her breasts, her belly. Fear was there, for she might fail again. And longing—oh, yes, longing rose in her, strong and demanding, longing that swirled through every shade of the rainbow, out into colors that had no names. She closed her eyes and felt those nameless colors sifting through her, drawn by the motions of his hands.

Her body had no doubts, felt no confusion. And this once, Maggie was willing to follow where her body led. She started to turn, to put her arms around him and her mouth on his.

He stopped her, pinning her firmly in place, her back to his front. "No," he said softly. "You're not in charge, Maggie. Whatever happens is up to me. You don't have to try, don't have to please anyone or do things right." One arm bound her to him at her waist. The other hand lifted and began unbuttoning her shirt. "It's all up to me, Maggie."

Up to him? Nothing she must try for, strive for...all she had to do was stand there and let him do whatever he wanted. The notion was alien. Frightening.

And desperately exciting.

Maggie stood very still. Outside, night crept closer, the shadows reaching out to each other, blending and merging as color fled. All those lost colors swam inside her now, warm and fluid and enticing.

Her shirt fell open. She felt the chill from the air near the window, and the heat from his hands. His fingers were callused, and the colors took on a sandpaper texture.

"Your breasts are so pretty." Luke whispered that into her ear, as if he were confiding a secret. "Soft and firm. Round and perfect."

Outside, the moon rested just above the dark shapes of the trees, fat and pale in a charcoal sky. Round and perfect...inside and out began to blend, dreamlike. Luke's scent and the feel of his hands on her skin. His words and the moon. The shadows and the heat gathering low in her belly—all of it reaching, coming together as he caressed her.

When he unzipped her jeans, she felt no alarm, no need to move. Until his hand slid inside.

Her body jolted.

"Shh." His breath came harder now, but his voice was easy. "Here, sweetheart, let me. Here's heat..." He slid a finger into the moisture he'd gathered from her and the moon, and the world slipped.

She reached behind her, grabbing him, afraid of falling in the suddenly unsteady world. "Luke!"

"I'm here, right here. So sweet," he murmured, and his other arm tightened around her. "I wish you could know how good it is to touch you like this...yes, move with me. Ride the feelings."

And she was moving. Moving with his hand, the dreamy languor burned away in the quick flash of need. *No control,* she thought with a spurt of panic. There was no controlling this, no choice, no safety. "I can't—Luke, I can't!"

"You don't have to do anything. Just let me...trust yourself, Maggie, trust what your body tells you..."

He continued to murmur praise and encouragement, but she lost the words as the colors merged, heat and hunger rocking her until there was only darkness, her pulse and his voice, his hand and the rising, clawing need—then the swift, hot explosion. Her body bucked. She cried out.

At last, he turned her in his arms, and held her. Just held her, while her legs trembled and the dimming of her senses gradually brightened once more. She put her arms around him. He felt so solid and real, the only reality that mattered.

Why, I love him, she thought.

He stroked her back. "Are you with me again?" he murmured.

His neck was damp, sweaty. He was breathing hard. She was limp, the needs of her body quiet, her mind ringing with astonishment.

One thing was plain. Luke wanted her. And she wanted him—more of him, all of him. Maggie tightened her arms around his neck and pressed a kiss to the salty place beneath his jaw.

He shuddered. "I want to, sweetheart. You can tell how much I want to, can't you? But..." Gently he disengaged her arms, sliding his hands down them to grasp her hands. He was smiling. Sort of. "I can't."

"Um..." Her gaze dipped down his body. "Excuse me, but that's not true."

"There's *can't* and there's can't." He lifted her hand to his mouth, pressed a kiss to it. He still smiled, but his eyes were sad. "I want you so much it's killing me. But I can't afford you, Maggie."

She stood quietly while he turned and walked away. But it wasn't his expert seduction or the sensory explosion he'd triggered that held her still. No, she was too busy arguing with herself to move.

She didn't love him. She couldn't. She was confusing lust and love, that was all—the man had just given her an incredible sexual experience, and her senses were overwhelmed. Disordered.

And that's all it had been, she thought with a little hitch of panic or pain. Sex. One-sided sex, at that. Not lovemaking.

And what the hell did he mean, he couldn't afford her?

Eleven

Maggie didn't see Luke again that night. She stayed up late writing in her journal, trying to make sense of her feelings, making a hundred useless guesses about what he had meant. Useless, because the only way she could know was to ask him. If she could find the courage.

She ended up oversleeping. It was nearly nine o'clock when she awoke with a huge weight pressing down on her chest. The sky had turned slate-gray, and the radio announced the arrival later that day of a winter storm.

Figures, Maggie thought as she pulled on her riding clothes. She could have used a good, head-clearing gallop today, wrist or no wrist. The only answers she'd found in her soul-searching last night involved seeing Luke again. Something it would be hard to avoid, she supposed, however much she wanted to.

Especially since part of her was dying to see him again.

Shaking her head at the perversity of her feelings, she went into the kitchen. Sarita was there. Alone.

"Luke wanted me to tell you he went to the feed store," she said, pulling the carton of eggs from the refrigerator.

Maggie's mood darkened. Maybe she wasn't sure if she wanted to see Luke or not. That didn't give him the right to take the decision out of her hands. "Oh, he did, did he?"

"I suppose he would have told you this himself if you shared his bed."

"Don't go there." Maggie grabbed a cup and poured coffee. "I am in no mood for being nagged about my sex life."

Sarita's plucked eyebrows shot up. "Are you sick?"

"No, I'm grouchy." She glanced at the eggs in Sarita's hand. "Don't bother with breakfast for me. I just want coffee."

"You *are* ill!" Sarita put the eggs down and hurried over. "There's a flu bug going around town."

Town, to those at the ranch, meant the dot-on-the-map called Bourne. Bourne had all the essentials of a small Texas town—a feed store, post office, Dairy Queen and bank. And not much more. "I am not sick," Maggie said with as much patience as she could summon. Sarita meant well, she reminded herself.

"Then you will eat. It will improve your mood."

"Not today. I'm running late." The more she thought about the way Luke had gone off to town without a word this morning, the madder she got. "Did Luke say when he'd be back?"

"Does anyone tell me anything around here?" She shrugged. "By noon, maybe. What's wrong with you two? You have had a fight?"

"Of course not," she said bitterly. "We can't fight from separate bedrooms, can we?" Or while he was in town. But once he returned, they could have a real knock-down-drag-out brawl.

She was beginning to think they would.

The phone rang. Seizing her chance to escape, Maggie quickly topped off her coffee and headed for the door.

Sarita's voice stopped her. "It's for you. Someone named Pamela."

By the time Luke unloaded the sacks of grain that had been his excuse to go to town, his mood was as foul as the weather. And the weather was damned nasty. Sleet slicked the roads and the ground, slapped around by a bad-tempered wind. It hissed at him as he sprinted from the stable to the house.

He went in through the kitchen door. Sarita wasn't there, but voices drifted in from the den. Women's voices. One of them was Maggie—there was no mistaking that low, husky voice. He didn't think the other was Sarita, though. He'd seen a sporty little convertible parked in front of the house when he got home. Apparently they had a visitor.

He scowled. He was in no mood for company—but there was something naggingly familiar about the other voice. Finally he shrugged and headed for the den.

Maggie sat on one of the leather couches, her leg tucked up beneath her there. She was wearing an old purple sweatshirt and yellow leggings.

She was talking to her cousin. His ex-wife.

He checked in the doorway. The two women looked up at the same time, but Pamela spoke first. "Luke, I—I hope you don't mind. I came to see Maggie."

"Why would I mind?" He made himself come into

the room. Pamela still liked pink, he saw; she was wearing a soft pink sweater with neatly pressed pink slacks. Her blond hair was shorter than it used to be, and the slim figure he remembered was a little too thin now. Her breasts were still full, though. And she still dramatized every word, every action. "Lousy day for a drive, though," he said mildly.

"I pointed that out," Maggie said. "When she called to tell me she was on her way."

There was something odd about Maggie's voice. He looked at her more closely. Her lips were thin, as if she was fighting to hold in hot words. Interesting. His eyebrows lifted.

"I don't care!" Pamela flung herself to her feet. "I came to—oh, but she won't listen to me." Emotion brought out the best in Pamela, as far as looks went. Her cheeks were pink with it, her eyes sparkled as she paced. "Not that I'm surprised. I know—God, how I know!— the way you affect women. But when Uncle Malcolm told me you'd married Maggie, I had to try."

At least she wasn't crying, Luke thought. Yet. "Wanted to warn her about me, did you? It's not necessary, you know. Maggie knows my sins almost as well as you do."

"Better, probably," Maggie said dryly. "You've pulled some stunts in the past nine years that Pamela might not be aware of."

Pamela stopped. Her pale hands clenched into fists at her side, and her thin figure fairly vibrated. "You think I'm amusing," she said in a low voice. "But then, you take pride in taking everything lightly, don't you, Maggie? Maybe you're better suited to Luke than I thought. Marriage was certainly one big joke to him."

"Pamela," he said wearily, "we've been divorced

more than nine times as long as we were married. Give it a rest."

She tipped her chin up. "Maybe you can forget the little angel I lost. I can't."

Just like that, he went hollow. And cold. So cold. "I've never forgotten. Or denied my share of the blame."

"Your share?" Pamela's voice rose. "If you'd had any heart at all—but no, you ran around. You were out every night, leaving me alone." Her voice hitched on a sob. "I was so alone, so scared. It was your fault, all your—"

"That's enough!" Maggie snapped, and stood.

Pamela was so astonished she stopped crying. "Maggie," she said, her voice filled with reproach, "are you taking his side? After what he did? I lost my baby!"

"Why must there be sides?" Maggie went to her and put a hand on her arm. "He lost his baby, too, Pamela."

"He never cared." She shrugged Maggie's hand off. "If he had, he wouldn't have treated me the way he did. And my baby—"

"No more. Do you hear me, Pamela? No more. You're right—Luke treated you badly. But he cared, deeply, about the baby. Why can't you admit that? For God's sake, you were the one who—"

Pamela gave a little cry and wrenched away. "I'm not going to listen to this! He's turned you against me." The tears were spilling now. "I'm leaving. I—I should have known better than to come." She darted for the couch, where a creamy cashmere coat had been tossed casually.

Luke's voice came out cool and distant. No surprise. He was slipping away even as he spoke, sliding down that cold, empty hole inside him. "You're too upset to drive. Especially when the roads are getting bad."

"I'm not staying," she spat, shrugging into her coat. "You can't make me stay."

"I'm not letting you drive on slick roads in this condition." He turned, started for the door. "I'll get one of the hands to take you in the pickup. It has four-wheel drive. Maggie—"

"Don't worry. I've got her keys."

He glanced over his shoulder. Sure enough, Maggie had appropriated her cousin's key ring, and Pamela was trying to snatch it back. With dim surprise, he felt his lips curve in a small smile. "Just what I was about to suggest."

He left to arrange for a driver for his ex-wife. When he came back, Maggie had her arm around Pamela and the two of them were speaking in low voices. "I'm sorry," he heard Pamela say. "I didn't mean to make a scene. I just...when I see him, it all comes back."

He understood what she meant only too well. "Tony's bringing the pickup around front. I'll get your car back to you tomorrow."

Pamela's gaze lifted to Luke, then flitted away. "I'm perfectly capable of driving myself."

"Maybe," Maggie said soothingly. "But I'd worry. Come on, now." She began steering them both for the front door. "Look on the bright side. This way you'll have someone to flirt with. Tony's cute."

Luke turned his back on the two women, tuning out their conversation. Instinctively he moved toward the fireplace, where a few desultory flames licked the logs someone had stacked haphazardly.

Maggie, probably. She enjoyed fires, but didn't have the knack of building them. He picked up a poker and drew the mesh screen aside, hoping to stir up more of a blaze. He shifted the top log, sending up a small shower of sparks.

God, he was cold.

"She's gone." Maggie sighed deeply. "Thank heavens. That was pretty awful."

"It wasn't fun." Heat from the fire touched the skin of the hand holding the poker, but went no further.

"Before Pamela called and said she was on her way here, I intended to fight with you."

A tiny lick of warmth curled his mouth up on one side. "You did, huh?" Carefully he put the poker back. "What were we going to fight about?"

"I hadn't decided."

At last he turned to face her. Her sweatshirt was big and loose and very purple. The daffodil-colored leggings fit like panty hose, curving intimately over her round, lovely bottom. All at once, his pulse leaped higher than the fire. He drew a ragged breath.

He knew how to banish the cold. Not permanently, but there was one sure way to drive it back to its hiding place, deep inside where he could mostly ignore it.

She tipped her head to one side consideringly. "You've got that look in your eyes."

No, dammit. He was not going to use Maggie for a quick fix. He ignored her comment. "Where's Sarita? It's lunchtime."

"I sent her home."

Worse than the physical hunger was another yearning, quieter than lust and a hell of a lot scarier. He turned away. "I guess I can rustle up a sandwich on my own. Why did you send Sarita home? Is she sick?"

"No, but the weather's getting bad, and...darn it. I promised myself I wouldn't do this—avoid the subject, I mean." She took a deep breath. "I sent her home so we could clear the air."

"I'm not interested in fighting right now. Sorry." He'd

nearly made it to the doorway, and was starting to breathe easier.

"Pamela's wrong. It wasn't your fault."

She'd stopped him cold. "Don't push this, Maggie."

"She wants to blame you so she won't have to blame herself. But she's the one who did it, Luke. *She* swallowed those pills."

He spun around—and lashed out with his hand, smashing a lamp to the floor. Maggie jumped. "You think I don't know that? God." A howl rose up inside, silent and deadly. He had to move, had to—grabbing for control, he started to pace. "I ignored her, ran around on her and she tried to kill herself. And killed our baby instead."

In the hush that fell he felt the silent howling rise, the frantic, empty burn of guilt. He stopped moving.

Maggie broke that silence. "I never believed that she really meant to kill herself. She didn't take enough pills. The doctor said her life was never in danger. It was a grab for attention, for sympathy, and probably a last-ditch effort to control you. You hurt her, yes, but she wasn't in love with you. She just couldn't stand to lose."

"So she was hurt and hysterical instead of in love and suicidal. What difference does it make?" His baby had died. Because of him. That was the truth, the only truth that mattered. "I didn't care about her. She was right about that. I married her because—"

"Because she was pregnant with your child," Maggie said quietly. "And you wanted your baby."

"She said she would deny I was the father if I didn't. I..." He ran a hand over his hair. "It was a hell of a basis for a marriage. Toward the end, I couldn't stand to be around her."

"I didn't like being around her myself back then."

Maggie came closer. "And she didn't trick me into marriage."

He looked at her sharply. "You knew about that?"

"Oh, yes." Her eyes were so sad and gentle. And warm. "She bragged about it when you were dating. Told me she'd tossed out her birth control pills. She also claimed you were crazy about her, that you only needed a little nudge. I think she convinced herself it was true. That's how she justified what she did."

"I was hot for her, all right." His laugh was bitter. "But when I found out she'd lied about being on the Pill…" His throat tightened. "I didn't want her anymore, but I wanted my baby."

"I know," she whispered. "I know you did."

"Pamela was a hysterical child in a woman's body. I knew that. God, who better? I grew up with just the sort of over-the-top emotional scenes she liked to treat me to. If I'd stayed with her that night… I should have guessed what she was capable of." Everything inside him seemed to be pulsing, like the ticking of a huge bomb.

Tentatively she put her hand on his arm. "You're not to blame for your baby's death, Luke."

His muscles went rigid. "You don't want to touch me now. I'm not safe."

"You won't hurt me." She sounded flat-out certain.

Her hand was small and steady and warm. So warm. He was shaking deep inside, and he needed that warmth badly. He made himself move slowly, but he couldn't stop himself from reaching for her, gripping her arms. "I won't hit you. But I will hurt you. Do you understand what I'm saying? If you don't get away from me right now, I will definitely hurt you, Maggie."

She didn't answer. Not in words. She just slid her arms

around his waist and put her sweet, warm body up against his and held him.

He shuddered once. And snapped.

One moment Maggie was holding Luke, aching for him, trying to press forgiveness inside him with her own body. The next, he was devouring her.

His mouth was hot and hard. Ruthless. He forced hers open and plunged inside.

Need. Had she ever felt such need before? Luke needed her. Desperately. A thrill raced up her spine, even as his hands raced over her body. She shivered. What was this? Fear? Lust? She needed—oh, she needed, too, needed to chase these demons. His or hers, it didn't matter.

His fingers dug into her hips, hard. Her arms went tight around him.

He tore his mouth away from hers and took it across her face, down her neck. His hands kneaded her bottom, and his leg came up between hers. A bolt of heat rocketed through her, shocking in its strength. She rocked against him. And whimpered.

"Maggie." His voice, hoarse, in her ear. "Maggie."

Just her name. That was all he said, but it was everything. "I'm here," she told him, just as he'd said to her last night. "I'm right here."

He gathered her tightly to him—then lifted her off her feet. In his arms. And he kissed her again, caught her mouth and held it while he moved with her—three quick steps, another, then they came down together on the couch. Leather, cool and slick beneath her back. His body, hard and hot atop hers, moving. His hands seeking, his mouth eating at hers. One hand cupped her low, between her legs. She gasped.

He raised his head. His eyes were dark, wild. "I can't

make it good for you this time.'' He grabbed the hem of her sweatshirt and jerked it up, and willy-nilly, she had to move to let him drag it over her head. ''I can't go slow. I can't. I'm sorry.''

She wasn't. Chilly air rushed over her exposed skin. She reached for him, needing the warmth and feel of him, but he held himself away, fumbling with her bra. The clasp defeated him, so he shoved it up.

His mouth caught the tip of one breast and sent her halfway mad. He sucked hard, almost too hard, and she made a little sound of protest. Already, though, he'd stopped. He was tugging at her leggings now, catching her panties with them. ''Maggie, dammit, these things are a bitch to get off.''

''When I put them on, I wasn't planning—'' Laughter rose, free and wild.

He had one of her legs free, and seemed satisfied with that because he stopped pulling at her pants, coming down fully atop her again, stopping her laughter with his mouth.

The denim of his jeans was rough against her most tender flesh. Deliciously rough. He pressed himself against her slowly, then more rhythmically. She yanked his shirt out of the waist of his jeans and sent her hands travelling over his back, crazy to feel him. Wanting his skin, his bare, entire body. Wanting him inside her, and wanting to somehow climb inside him, too.

She pulled her mouth away long enough to gasp his name. ''Your jeans,'' she added.

He cursed, low and heartfelt, and shifted to reach in his pocket. He pulled out his wallet, took something from it, and tossed the wallet on the floor. Then he was kissing her again, kissing her as if he couldn't stand to stop.

''Maggie,'' he said, and ran his tongue around her ear.

"I can't wait. Do you understand?" He touched her face, and his hand shook. Then he lifted himself slightly, and his movements told her he was putting on a condom.

Of course Luke would use protection, she thought. Sadness dimmed the reckless urgings of her body. Always, no matter how urgent his need, he would take the time to slide that thin layer of latex between himself and heartbreak—because that's how he would see the chance of starting a child. She remembered the tears on his cheeks nine years ago, and felt her own heart break a little. Her hands turned tender. She stroked him gently, and when he used his knee to urge her legs apart, she opened to him.

Then he thrust inside, and she forgot everything in sheer wonder at how they fit, how hot and big and perfect he felt inside her.

He thrust hard once. Again. Then something seemed to catch him up and throw him straight into a gallop, and he moved in her fast and hard. She groaned and caught his rhythm and they were together, bodies bucking, her hands going crazy as if she could grab every part of him at once.

Like a slap, her climax hit her, buckled her, sending her voice into a high, thin cry and her mind flying. He ground himself into her and groaned out her name. His body jerked and arched. And he collapsed on top of her.

His head was on her shoulder, and she heard his breath and felt it, too. He was still inside her. Little aftershocks skittered through her body. Her bra was up under her armpits and her mind felt dreamy and white, as if all the colors had merged. How strange, she thought, fingering the damp hair at his nape, that she could float when she was anchored, firmly and physically, to the earth. To him.

He moved slightly, groaned, then propped himself up

on his elbows. His eyes were soft. He touched her cheek. "I was going to apologize," he said. "Until you exploded."

She felt a silly smile stretch her face. "I did, didn't I?"

"I'm not going to be able to let you alone now, you know." He sounded as if he was trying to speak lightly, but it didn't come out that way. "If you won't come to my bed, I'll move into yours."

Her heartbeat, which had just settled down, quickened again. She wanted, badly, to tell him she loved him. But he'd run fast and hard in the other direction if she did. "Good idea. I might need more practice with, um, explosions."

He studied her face for a moment, then, slowly, his face relaxed into a grin. "Speaking as your trainer," he said, running a hand along her side, "I'd say you're ready for the next lesson. And so am I."

Twelve

December light. There was a clarity to it, Luke thought, but little color and less warmth.

The big bay mare he was brushing snorted and shifted her weight. Muscles moved beneath Luke's hands, and he smiled. There was warmth here, in the smooth flank, the steamy, impatient breath of the beast.

His gaze drifted deeper into the stable, where Maggie stood, tethered by the phone cord, yet still in motion— pacing, twining the cord around her fingers, running a hand through her short, messy hair. She was dressed for riding in boots, stretch pants and an old red sweater with a small hole in one shoulder. Emotions chased themselves across her face as naturally as dogs chase rabbits— laughter, doubt, affection. She paused, head cocked as if listening, then shrugged.

There, too, was warmth.

He watched the quick motions of her hands while his

own went about their business automatically, smoothing
Foxfire's winter coat with long strokes. Maggie's cast
was due to come off in two weeks, on Christmas Eve.
The swelling was gone, and she used that hand almost
normally now.

She still wore his ring on the wrong hand.

His gaze fell on his own hand as he smoothed the
brush across the mare's withers. Gold gleamed on the
third finger on his left hand, and pain twisted in his chest.
He'd fooled himself royally, hadn't he? Telling himself
he was rushing Maggie to the altar so he could help her,
make up to her for what he hadn't remembered doing
that night in Phoenix.

Oh, yeah. That had to have been one of the best lies
he'd ever told. He'd married her because he wanted to
have her. To keep her. And that was a folly so huge he
couldn't much blame himself for hiding the truth behind
a tangle of rationalizations.

Inevitably, his attention drifted back to Maggie. She
stood with her back mostly to him now. The sweet curve
of her cheek fascinated him as much as the curves
snugged by her riding pants.

There was heartache. Not yet, but on its way.

For the past nine nights, she'd slept in his bed—when
they got around to sleeping, that is. She'd given herself
to him as if she'd been made for loving. For *his* loving.
But it was in the quiet moments afterward when she
wound more and more thin, unbreakable strands around
his heart. When she lay in his arms and he felt her heart
beat against his. When everything about her—the sleepy
smile on her lips, her limp body and glowing eyes—
spoke of trust. Sweet, complete trust. In him.

He couldn't regret what he'd done. Not now, at least,

and not for himself. Some things were worth almost any price. Any cost.

Maggie was an intelligent woman, and not self-destructive. She knew him as well as anyone…better, perhaps, than anyone. The only way she could give him her trust would be if she'd managed to withhold her heart. So he knew she'd accepted him as a lover, that she cared about him as a friend…and wasn't in love with him at all.

Which was good, he reminded himself, ignoring the tightness in his chest as he set the brush down and pulled a hoof pick from his pocket. He didn't want her love. This way, most of the hurt would be his. This way, he couldn't break her heart.

She hung up the phone and came toward him. "That was my mom. She and my dad give this big party every year—the high heels and glitter kind, you know? Very dressy. She, uh, wants us to come. I didn't know if you'd want to, so I told her I'd call her back. It's this Saturday. It will be pretty stuffy. You'd probably be bored."

"But she asked, and you want to go."

Her eyes held a trace of anxiety. "I think she argued with my father about inviting us, though she wouldn't admit it. That's really hard for her to do."

"Then we'll go." He was glad he could do this for her. He'd do a lot more, if he could. "I warn you, though—I draw the line at wearing high heels. A little glitter, maybe."

She laughed and hooked her arm through his. "I don't know—I think you'd look sexy in heels." She slid a lash-lowered glance over his body. "Of course, I think you look sexy in anything. Or nothing at all."

"You're trying to make me crazy, aren't you?" For the past four days, Maggie had had her period, and she was one of those women who were hit hard by cramps. His body had felt the effects of abstinence almost immediately. But she'd let him know that morning that she was feeling better. Much better.

"Yep," she said cheerfully. "How am I doing?"

"I don't think anyone is in the tack room right now. Of course, it doesn't have a lock, but if we put you up against the door and—"

Her laugh was free, happy, and incredibly sexy. "Lust later. Lunch now, or Sarita will kill us."

They started for the house, her hand tucked firmly under his arm. What was it, he wondered, that made one woman special, different from all the others? There had been women more beautiful than Maggie. Sweet women, spicy women, women both gentle and tart-tongued. He'd cared about them all, in his way.

But his way had always been temporary. What he felt for Maggie was different—stronger, sweeter. A helluva lot scarier.

But *he* wasn't any different.

"We could get away with being late for lunch," he suggested. "Sarita is pleased with us right now for having finally moved your things into my room."

"I am not ducking into the tack room for a quickie. That would be…tacky."

His lips quivered. "And your point is?"

She chuckled. After a moment she said, "Luke?"

"Yeah?" Her hip bumped his thigh lightly with every step. It was a good feeling.

"I was thinking. Mom believes our marriage is for real. I feel guilty about fooling her. Maybe I should explain to her…you know, that it's temporary."

Her head was down as if she were studying her footing on the bare earth in front of the stable. All he could see was her shiny hair, the unrevealing line of her forehead curving into her cheek. And that little hole in the shoulder of her sweater, where the seam was unraveling.

"Yes," he said, those thin strands around his heart squeezing tight, tighter. "Probably you should."

It was nearly midnight when Maggie tucked the presents she'd just finished wrapping under the tree. She sat back on her heels to admire the sight.

It was a great tree. Last weekend, she and Jeremy had wrestled four strings of multicolored lights through the branches in spite of millions of needles determined to prick and obstruct them. They'd hung balls and bells and icicles, candy canes and reindeer, elves and Santas and an Obi-Wan Kenobi figurine. When you pushed a button on Obi-Wan's back, he advised you to trust the Force.

Luke hadn't complained about the tree. He hadn't said one word about it. Not one. He'd left the house while they decorated it, and ever since he'd done a top-notch job of ignoring the presence of an eight-foot Christmas tree in his den.

Would he even notice the presents she'd left there for him?

With a sigh, she stood. The air was chilly, so she tightened the belt on her robe, then paused to stroke the collar. It was wonderfully warm and fluffy. And red—a bright, happy lipstick-red. Luke had given it to her the day after she'd tried out her black satin nightgown on him. He was crazy about the nightgown, he'd said, and hoped she'd wear it for him often—under the robe. He knew how she hated to be cold.

The sweetness of it made her eyes sting even as she smiled. He was a good man. A good friend, as well as a lover. When she'd been huddled on the couch, riding out a miserable session of cramps, he'd brought her ibuprofen and a heating pad.

And yet, she wished he'd waited and given her the robe for Christmas. It was silly, but she wished it had been a Christmas present.

Patience, she reminded herself. He'd been hurting a long time, blaming himself and hating Christmas for a long time. She couldn't wish away his problems. All she could do was love him, and wait.

And prod him a little now and then with things like Christmas trees in his den. She was smiling, anticipating, when she reached the bedroom she now shared with him, but her smile slipped away when she opened the door. The room was dark. Disappointment flooded her.

He must have gotten tired and gone to sleep. She bit her lip. Why had she stayed up wrapping presents so late?

She shut the door quietly behind her. And sighed. It was late, she reminded herself. And he'd put in a long day. And—and why couldn't he have been as eager as she was to celebrate the end of her period? She toed off her slippers and padded across the thick carpet, slipping out of her robe when she reached the bed.

Feeling mistreated, she slid between the covers, careful not to wake him. The moment her head touched the pillow, a large, warm arm curled around her. "Come here," Luke murmured.

She did.

His lovemaking had begun to grow familiar, but always before, there had been light—from the fireplace, a lamp or dawn sneaking in the windows. Darkness created a different sort of intimacy, a place of hushed sighs, where the scent and texture of his skin aroused her as much as the touch of his hand.

Always before, there had been words between them,

too. Tender or teasing, words that linked their minds as
well as their bodies. Tonight, he was silent. He loved her
slowly, carefully, sending her over the first peak with the
magic of his hands and mouth. While she still floated,
stunned, he slid inside her. And showed her how lovely
it could be to move slowly, to wrap herself around him
and rock him while he stroked her, the world dark and
silent around them. Until at last they eased over the top
together…and settled gently back to earth in each other's
arms.

It wasn't until her heartbeat steadied and his breathing
slowed that she realized her cheeks were wet.

Tears? She touched her cheek, amazed. But she never,
ever cried. She didn't know how. And she wasn't sad.
She just…oh, she wished, she did wish, she could tell
him she loved him.

Maybe she should, she thought as her cheeks dried in
the chilly air. Maybe holding the words back wasn't instinct, but cowardice.

"Even the weather's cooperating," Maggie said, fighting to get an earring in place as she clicked across the
kitchen floor in her only pair of high heels. "I guess my
father put in an order for tonight, and God filled it."

Sarita scolded her in Spanish for disrespect to the
Deity, then switched to English. "Here, give me that."

"I think the hole's started to close up," she said, obe-
diently handing one earring to Sarita.

"Then we will open it again. There."

"Ouch." Maggie winced, then shook her head so she
could feel the tiny drop move. "How do I look?"

"Men will suffer," Sarita announced with satisfaction,
and held out her hand. "Give me the other one now."

"I hope so. I suffered enough to look this way." She'd

done it all—a facial, a bout with a curling iron and a painstaking time in front of the mirror with brushes, powders and tubes. Her dress was short and sleek and silk, a blue so dark the color showed only in the shimmer.

If it had left been up to her, the dress would still be hanging in the snooty little dress shop where she'd found it. She wasn't sure she could pull off something this sophisticated. But she'd gone shopping with her sister-in-law-to-be, and Claire had insisted this was the dress for her.

In addition to being drop-dead gorgeous and a financial whiz, Claire had excellent taste. If she'd been really sweet, too, Maggie might have hated her. Instead she was a little tart, and a lot of fun.

She smiled. Think of that—she was going to have a sister-in-law.

For a while, anyway. Her smile faded.

"Got it." Sarita drew back. "Now you are glad you listened to your *cuñada,* right? You look terrific."

"Right." Maggie smoothed her hands down the little dab of skirt the dress provided. "It *is* short, isn't it?"

"Yes." Sarita nodded with satisfaction. "Men *will* suffer. They will trip over their tongues."

"Gross." That came from Jeremy, who lounged in the doorway. Sarita had agreed to stay tonight so he wouldn't be alone. Not that it would have bothered him, but Maggie hadn't felt right about leaving him here.

Maggie turned. "You don't like the dress?"

"The dress is fine. Foxy," he said, nodding judiciously. "The gross part will be all those dragging tongues wiping up the floor."

Maggie laughed. "You're right. That is gross." She felt pretty tonight, a little giddy. There was only one more opinion she needed. "Where's Luke?"

"In his study," Jeremy said. "He's doing, like, business stuff on his computer."

Her heart danced happily as she started down the hall. She wanted to preen for Luke, to show off her new dress. She knew he'd compliment her—and she knew he would mean it. Luke made her feel beautiful when she was hugging a heating pad to her aching tummy.

Oh, he was a good man. A wonderful man. Today a present had appeared under the tree that she hadn't put there—a big, gold box wrapped with more haste than skill. The tag said it was for Jeremy, from Luke.

She'd hugged herself for sheer joy when she saw it. She didn't care if he bought her a Christmas present. Well, not much, anyway. The important thing was that he'd set aside his own feelings to buy something for the boy she was sure he loved like a son.

She was halfway down the hall when the phone rang.

"For you, Maggie!" Sarita called.

She checked impatiently, glancing at her watch. There was time. She'd gotten ready early. She turned around and found that Sarita had brought the phone to her. "Thanks." She took it. "This is Maggie."

"Margaret West?" an unfamiliar voice asked.

A little thrill went through her. *Margaret West.* She grinned, amused at herself. Next thing you knew, she'd be writing it out and drawing little hearts around it, like any giddy teenager. "I prefer Maggie, but yes, that's me."

"This is Grace Hammond. I need to ask you something rather personal, I'm afraid. I'm Jeremy's case worker, and I'm worried about him."

Jeremy lay flat on his stomach, admiring the lights, the tree—and the packages under it.

Five of them were for him. Five! Excitement wiggled through him. There were three packages wrapped in Star Wars paper from Maggie—the square one with the huge green bow, and one he was afraid was clothes. It was that kind of box. And one more, a funny-shaped package with a lopsided bow. The tag on that one read, "Dear Jeremy—if you mess with this it will explode and I will hear it and come kill you. Love, Maggie."

Of course, females used that "love" word a lot. It didn't mean anything, not really. But he kind of liked it that she'd signed the tag that way.

He *had* messed with the package, of course, trying to feel the shape beneath the layers of paper. So far he hadn't been able to figure out what it was.

In addition to the presents from Maggie, there was one that rattled when he shook it. That was from Sarita. And a great, huge box that didn't weigh much at all, wrapped in gold foil.

That one was from Luke.

He gazed at the big gold box, wondering about it. Wondering about a lot of things. His stomach felt tight and jumpy. Finally the feelings squirming around inside him got too active for him to stay still another second. He sprang to his feet and headed for the kitchen. Sarita would know where the wrapping paper and stuff was. He had presents to wrap, too.

They weren't much. He felt a tug of worry about that. He'd managed to save twenty-two dollars, but twenty-two dollars didn't go far.

He was on his way to his room with paper, tape and ribbon when he saw Maggie opening the door to Luke's office. She didn't see him—she was looking straight ahead. For some reason he stopped. Maybe it was the look on her face, all serious-like. "Do you know where Jeremy is?" he heard her ask Luke.

Luke answered, but his voice was too low for Jeremy to catch it all. He heard something about "packages," though.

"Good." Maggie went in, closing the door behind her.

Jeremy frowned. Probably they were just going to kiss and stuff. There'd been a lot of that going on lately, and it made him feel funny, but good. He liked the idea that they were stuck on each other.

Maybe she'd closed the door so they could talk about important stuff, though. Like packages. And what was in that big gold box.

He would listen just for a minute, he decided. If they were getting all sweaty over each other, he'd go away. He didn't want to mess with their privacy or anything. Putting down the wrapping paper, he snuck up on the closed door, and listened.

"Do you know where Jeremy is?" Maggie asked.

Luke turned from his computer to smile at her. "I think he's shaking packages," he said dryly.

"Good." She closed the door behind her. "Luke, I just talked to Jeremy's case worker, Grace Hammond. She asked me…" Maggie bit her lip. This was hard. She didn't know how to tackle it except head-on, though. "She thinks Jeremy is expecting you to adopt him. That that's the reason we got married—to make it easier for you to adopt him."

The shock on his face couldn't have been greater if she'd slid a knife between his ribs. "Good God." He shoved his chair back so hard it nearly toppled when he stood. "Where did he get a damnfool idea like that?" he demanded. "What have you been telling him?"

"Not a blasted thing." She put her hands on her hips—or tried to. The one with the cast slid off.

"Never mind." He scrubbed his hair back from his face. "It's not you. It's me. God." He paced out from behind his desk. "I should have seen...what did she say to you? Maybe she's wrong. Or maybe this is her doing. If she's said anything to him, put ideas in his head—"

"Luke." She shook her head. "You can't fix this by fixing blame."

He stopped at the window, his head bent, rubbing his neck. "It's not blame so much as...I have to know where he got this stupid idea. I have to understand. What did she tell you?"

Her heart went out to him. He cared so much. However blind and stupid he might be about it, he cared. "He's been asking her questions about adoption and the law. Last month he wanted to know if a single man could adopt a kid. She was sure he meant you, but he insisted he was asking for a friend, and she let it go at that. She told him the courts preferred to place children with married couples, thinking that was the gentlest way of letting him down. Then you got married. And today she met with him the way she does once a month, and he asked her a 'hypothetical question.' He wanted to know how long people had to be married before they could adopt— if they wanted to."

He didn't move, didn't speak for a long moment. Then he raised his head to stare blindly out the window. "I didn't know," he said at last. "I didn't have a clue what was going on in his head."

She went to him, put her hand on his arm. Should she say it? Would it make things better or worse if she said exactly what she thought? She took a deep breath and plunged ahead. "Parents don't always know. They guess, they do their best, but they don't always know."

Luke shook her off. "I'm not his father. Or anyone else's. I'm careless about a lot of things, but not that. Never that."

"Why?" she asked fiercely. "You'd be a wonderful father. You feel like a father now, whether you want to admit it or not. You *love* that boy. Maybe adoption never occurred to you, but now that it has—"

"For God's sake, Maggie, stop being such an ass."

She took a deep breath. "I'm trying to hang on to my temper here, but you are not making it easy."

"If you don't want to be called an ass, don't act like one! Can you see me as a *father?*" He started to pace again. "There is no way I will put a child through the game of musical moms that I like to call my childhood."

Here was the bitterness he'd never let her see before. "You aren't your father."

He laughed, but it broke in the middle. "I'm just like him. I've heard it all my life. I like women the way he did—in the plural. Always in the plural. My brothers, my mother, my stepmoms—they've all pointed out how much I'm like him. I proved them right when I ran around on Pamela, didn't I? I proved how unfit I am to be a husband—or a father."

"Don't you dare use that as an excuse! Maybe you weren't ready to be a husband back then—"

"I'm still not."

He said it so quietly. So certainly. The hurt started, a small, quiet rip deep inside. Still, she pushed on. "You've acted like a husband to me, Luke. A good one. You're a good man."

He looked suddenly weary. Bewildered. "How can you say that? Maggie, you *know* me. Hell, when I asked you to marry me, you wanted to know if I'd ever been faithful to any woman for more than a week. I didn't answer you then, but I will now. The answer is no. I haven't.''

Stubbornly she insisted, ''You hadn't *then*. You have now.''

''I gave you my word. I've kept it. But this is temporary, this arrangement of ours, isn't it? Do you really think you could trust me for the long haul?'' He shook his head. ''I don't trust myself. How can you?''

Her heart was pounding so hard it seemed to be shaking her from the inside out. This was her chance, the moment she'd been waiting for. The moment to speak the words pressing up, trying to force themselves past the fear clogging her throat. Maggie saw that as clearly as she'd ever seen a jump come suddenly upon her while galloping down a twisting lane. She saw it—and shied.

''We're getting off the subject,'' she said shakily. ''You want to look me in the eye and tell me you don't love Jeremy? That you don't already think of him as a son?''

He did look her in the eye. His eyes were clear, letting her see the pain, the soul-deep regret. Making her sure, suddenly, that holding the words back hadn't hidden them from him. ''Sometimes love isn't enough.''

Thirteen

—————

They went to her parents' party. It was the last place Luke wanted to be, but Maggie insisted. He suspected she didn't want to explain to Sarita and Jeremy why they'd changed their minds. He didn't blame her. He hadn't wanted to face Jeremy, either. When Sarita told them he was in his room wrapping presents, Luke had grabbed at the excuse to avoid facing the boy he couldn't have for a son.

Sooner or later, though, he would have to talk to Jeremy. What in the world was he going to say? What could possibly be wise enough, smart enough, to matter when stacked up against the destruction of dreams?

So why not go to the damned party? It couldn't be any worse than spending the evening avoiding each other at home. Maybe it would help to get out among people, forcing them to act as if everything was fine. They were both good at that. She hid behind humor while he used charm, but when you got right down to it, their masks weren't all that different.

But neither of them bothered with those masks when they were alone together, in his truck. It was a decades' long drive into the city, made in silence and regrets.

They arrived fashionably late. And found a few surprises waiting for them.

The presence of Jacob and his fiancée at the party was the first shock. Probably, Luke thought, sipping the sparkling water he'd requested, it shouldn't have been. He knew Jacob and Malcolm Stewart had had business dealings, and Jacob frequently attended this sort of affair.

The other surprises were less pleasant. Like the one who had latched onto his arm and was rubbing her breast against it right now. "Still not interested in subtlety, are you, Mary Jeanne?" he said mildly.

"I don't see much point in it." Her mouth drooped. "You're not going to tell me you do, all of a sudden?"

A mouth like hers was made for pouting, he thought. Among other things. "It does seem to be called for, with my new in-laws watching. Not to mention my wife."

"She's in the other room, honey," Mary Jeanne assured him.

So she was. So she had been for thirty minutes now—in any room other than the one he was in. Jacob, however, was right here. He stood ten feet away, watching Luke with iced-over eyes. No one, Luke thought, could glare quite the way his big brother did—without an ounce of expression on his face.

He made a bet with himself. Five minutes. He'd give his brother five minutes before hauling him away. "I thought you and Maggie were friends."

"I like her well enough." She looked honestly puzzled.

"You don't consider it tacky to come on to me in her parents' home?"

She giggled. "Darling, I live for tacky."

Yeah. And she did "tacky" so well. He looked at her and wondered why he'd ever bothered.

Mary Jeanne was only one of the unpleasant surprises his in-laws had had waiting for him, though. Someone had gone to a lot of trouble, he thought, to make him feel at home. There were two other women here who might be called old flames of his.

Mary Jeanne murmured something about how warm it was in here. Luke agreed absently. Jacob was headed his way.

Under five minutes, he thought. He won.

"Excuse me," Jacob said to Mary Jeanne with chilly courtesy. "I need to talk to my brother a moment. A family matter." His eyes flicked to Luke's. "Outside."

"I need to talk to you, Daddy. In your study."

Maggie's father spared her a glance. "You're interrupting, Margaret." Immediately he returned his attention to the business of socializing with the people who mattered—people he either did business with, or might want to do business with someday.

Malcolm Stewart wasn't a tall man, or especially handsome. His hair was thinning, and his features were unremarkable. He had presence, though, the kind bestowed by intelligence and supreme self-confidence. His air of certainty had always made Maggie feel small, awkward and unsure; in the past, a dismissal like the one he'd just handed her would have quelled her. She would have stammered an apology and tried harder to please him.

Not tonight. "I don't give a holy hoot. I need to talk to you *now.*"

He gave her another glance. Irritation flickered in gray-blue eyes, but he nodded. "Very well. Excuse me, please."

The temperature had dropped. That was obvious as soon as Luke stepped out on the back patio. It was dark and private here, with the sound of the wind shivering its way through the nude branches that stretched over the eastern half of the porch. The sky was a murky black, and the air was cold and damp. Luke faced out, toward the darkness.

Behind him were the sounds of the party, suddenly muffled as Jacob closed the glass door. And his brother's voice.

"Damned if I can figure out what's going on in your head tonight, letting that woman hang all over you. It isn't like you."

"I'd say it's exactly like me."

Jacob sighed. "Looks like I'm going to have to pound you after all."

Luke thought about obliging Jacob. A brawl might clear the air. A couple of smart-ass remarks occurred to him, the kind guaranteed to provoke his big brother.

Only he was too damned tired for it. For any of this. He moved farther into the shadows. At the edge of the patio a decorative railing stopped him and he put his hand on it, curling his fingers around cold iron. "If you like. Or you might try tossing some advice my way, instead of a punch."

He could feel his brother's surprise almost as clearly as he felt his own. He hadn't intended to say that.

"You haven't asked me for advice since you were fifteen," Jacob said, a thread of humor in his voice. "And you didn't take it then."

Luke smiled wearily at the darkness. "As I recall, I wanted to know how to juggle two girlfriends, since I couldn't make up my mind between Peggy Armstead and Julie Price. Your advice was, 'don't.'"

"It was good advice." Jacob came up beside him. He thrust his hands into his pockets and looked out at the night, too. "Still is. What the hell is going on, Luke?"

He surprised himself a second time. "I'm in love with Maggie."

Jacob's curse was low, heartfelt and far from flattering. "Claire said you were, but I didn't believe her."

Luke shifted restlessly. "Women always seem to know. Maybe they smell it on us."

"Maybe. Is that what has you acting the fool tonight, then?" He shook his head. "Making Maggie jealous is not the way to win her, Luke. If you want her to return your feelings—"

"No," Luke said. His hand tightened on the railing. "The problem is that she already does."

Her father's study was tasteful, expensive and efficient. He had everything he needed to conduct business here, but seldom did. He preferred his corner office in the high-rise downtown. Maggie stopped halfway into the room and turned to face him, feeling like a long shot contender challenging the champ.

He closed the door behind him but stayed near it, a clear signal that he intended this conversation to be brief. "All right, Margaret. You have what you wanted. I've deserted my guests to hear what you consider more important than good manners."

"Your guests are what I'd like to discuss."

His eyes flickered away, then back to her. "I don't

believe it is any of your concern whom your mother and I invite to our house.''

That brief wavering of his gaze gave her great satisfaction. It was a small enough show of uncertainty, but more than she'd ever wrested from him before. ''It is when you compose the guest list with the intention of embarrassing me and my husband.''

''Your *husband* is managing his embarrassment, and yours, quite well without assistance.''

Her palms were damp. She looked down at them, waiting for the sickness in the pit of her stomach to ease. ''You invited her,'' she said quietly. ''The woman who's draped herself all over Luke. She isn't part of your circle.''

''Simply because you aren't acquainted with everyone here—''

''Oh, I'm acquainted with Mary Jeanne,'' Maggie said. ''I've run into her at a number of shows. She's part of the same set as a couple of the other women here tonight—women who ride a little, and party a lot. I'm not sure you ever met them before, though.'' Her hands clenched into fists. ''You invited them because of Luke. Because at some point he was—involved—with them. I don't know how you found out—''

''It wasn't difficult. Luke West has always conducted his affairs openly.''

There was a tight little hitch of hurt in her chest. ''Then you admit it. You invited them here to punish me.''

His eyes widened. ''No. No! How could you think that?''

''What else am I supposed to think?'' She bit her lip. Dang it, she wasn't going to start sniffing. ''You're furious with me for defying you.''

"Maggie." He gave his head a single, bewildered shake. She could have sworn he looked hurt. "Isn't a father allowed to worry about his child? Of course I'm unhappy about your impulsive marriage. I know why you did it—to strike back at me. To make a point. I suppose…" He ran a hand over his hair. "I may have been too harsh with you. Too demanding. I may have pushed you into that man's arms with my unyielding attitude." He sighed. "Your mother certainly thinks so."

Something was wrong with her eyes. They were stinging like crazy and making everything blurry. "Mother said that?"

He grimaced. "Repeatedly. She didn't approve of my plans tonight, either. But I thought…I hoped that if you saw West clearly, if you understood the kind of man he is, you would leave him. I—I don't want you to be hurt."

He'd invited Luke's old flames because, in his ham-handed, idiotic way, he was looking out for her. "Oh, Daddy." Her voice broke, caught between laughter and tears. "Who would have thought you and he would have so much in common? He's trying to accomplish the same thing."

"Let me see if I understand what you've been telling me," Jacob said. He was leaning against the railing. "You were letting that female paw you so Maggie would fall out of love with you."

"That's pretty much it." Luke moved from one shadow to another, unable to be still. Baring his soul to his brother had been one of his more stupid ideas.

"You're hurting her in order to keep from hurting her."

Put that way, it didn't sound too bright. "I'm not sure

it worked," he admitted, pausing. "But I'm damned if I know what I'm supposed to do."

"The hurting her part worked just fine, I'd say. I haven't seen her since that redhead draped herself around you."

"Maybe." Luke sighed. "Or maybe she's trying to show me that she trusts me."

Jacob snorted. "And this doesn't tell you something?"

Luke faced his brother, legs spread. "Are you saying that all of a sudden you do trust me? You think I'll be faithful? That wasn't your original reaction."

"That was before I knew you had feelings for her." He shook his head. "You're an idiot. You gave up smoking when you turned twenty. You've got the willpower to change a bad habit if you want to badly enough. If you're in love with Maggie, you'll want to."

Luke stared at his brother incredulously. "That's the sum total of your advice? I'm supposed to give up women the same way I quit smoking?"

"Pretty much."

"Thanks. That helps a lot."

"Women are just a habit for you. A long-standing one, I'll admit." Jacob looked away, shrugging uncomfortably. "Goes back to your childhood, I guess."

"I wasn't that precocious," Luke said dryly.

"I'm not talking about sex. I'm talking about how you are with women. You've always liked them, enjoyed them. You got along with all our stepmothers because you blamed our father for everything."

Luke's jaw tightened. "He made it easy to do that."

"Yeah, that was the easy way. For you, anyway. I had other ways of dealing with things, but for you, it was easiest to put all the blame in one place. You got in the habit of caring a little about a lot of women because it was safer than caring a lot about one woman, and getting your heart broken. Like it was the day your mother walked out.''

Luke felt a wild urge to swing at Jacob. His hand clenched. ''He didn't give her much choice. He was running around on her—''

''Maybe. Or maybe that was all in her head. She was jealous, Luke. Sick-jealous. You know that. She thought he was cheating on her every time he smiled at another woman. Look,'' he said roughly, ''I'm not excusing him. I'm just saying it wasn't as black-and-white as—''

The glass door slid open with a jerk. Luke pivoted, hoping whoever had interrupted them was a man. He really needed to sock someone.

Maggie stood in the rectangular spill of light, her skin two shades paler than it should be. ''Luke. Thank God I found you. Sarita called. Jeremy took Samson. He's run away.''

Fourteen

"**H**ow fast will this thing go?" Luke asked, leaning forward. He and Maggie were in the back seat of Jacob's car. Jacob had insisted they take it, since they wouldn't all fit in Luke's pickup—and, though neither he nor Claire rode, they were definitely going, too. Claire sat up front with Jacob, not a hair out of place on her beautiful head. She'd left the party without stopping for her coat or asking a single question.

"One-twenty," Jacob answered. "But not in town." The big car pulled away from the driveway with a smooth surge of power. "Now. Who's Jeremy?"

Maggie made a muffled sound that might have been a laugh. Or incipient hysteria. Luke squeezed her hand. "One of the boys I've been teaching to ride. I..." He looked down at the floorboard, at his feet planted wide there. He felt Maggie's hand in his, small and soft and strong.

Luke swallowed hard. "I've been thinking about adopting him."

"Of course I'm coming." Maggie pulled on her other boot.

"Forget it." Luke grabbed his coat. They'd both changed quickly into riding gear—arguing the whole time. "You've got a broken arm."

"The cast comes off in two weeks."

"It isn't off now. You're staying here."

"Like hell I am." She grabbed his arm when he tried to shove past her. "Luke, you can leave without me. It won't keep me from following."

She saw real fury in his eyes then. She didn't blame him for that, or for his silence ever since he'd heard everything Sarita had told her.

Jeremy had left a note. It didn't say much, just that he knew when he wasn't wanted, and that he'd get Samson back to Luke. They'd both known what it meant. Somehow, he had heard them talking about adoption—and he'd heard Luke's violent reaction.

She swallowed guilt and fear and met Luke's anger with her own determination. "We need everyone looking who can handle a horse. I won't slow you down, Luke. I know it's my fault—"

He grabbed her arms. "Where did you get a stupid idea like that?"

"I should have made sure," she said miserably. "I didn't see him, but I should have made sure he wasn't close enough to overhear."

He shook his head. "I was the one who kept saying adopting him was crazy. That's why he ran away."

"You didn't know he was there! You—oh. Oh, we are a pair, aren't we?" She rubbed her chest, where she could swear she felt humor struggling to loosen the knots tied by pain, fear and urgency. It made for a funny kind of ache. "All right. I won't blame me, if you won't blame you."

"Deal." His smile came and went swiftly. "Come on."

The weather was worsening. There was a cold front moving in—and pushing a storm ahead of it. A cold drizzle met them when they went outside. So did Roscoe, an older man who worked for Luke. He handed Luke Gotcha Girl's reins.

She gave Luke a quick, questioning glance. The mare had heart, but she was jumpy and inexperienced.

"She's young," he said tersely, swinging up into the saddle. "But she's fast." He looked at Roscoe. "Saddle Dandy."

Maggie made her way through half a dozen mounted men milling around in front of the stable. She saw slickers, cowboy hats and Western saddles; quarter horses in shades of bay and brown, and one calm-eyed Morgan. Luke's neighbors had turned out to search. The law had been notified, too, of course, but the deputies would be searching the roads.

Luke thought he knew where Jeremy had gone. The boy had been fascinated by tales of the outlaws who'd once holed up in a cave on the far western edge of Luke's land. Jeremy had pestered Luke more than once to let him explore the cave—and been refused. It wasn't safe. The walls of the cave were mostly earth, an unstable hidey-hole cut from the high banks of a creek.

And, just before reaching the ranch, they'd gotten another call. Samson had wandered into the stable area of one of Luke's neighbors—the one nearest the cave.

In the middle of several tons of restless horseflesh stood a tall man in evening clothes. Jacob was passing out cell phones. She had no idea where he'd gotten them.

While Luke divided the men into teams of two, Maggie and Roscoe worked feverishly to tack up Dandy. She swung onto his back there in the stable. He was fidgety, unhappy with her decision to leave the comfort of the stable at this hour. Wait until he found it was raining, she thought grimly. Dandy didn't like rain—unless he was competing. All he cared about then was getting ahead of any horse foolish enough to be in front of him.

"All right," she heard Luke call as she urged Dandy forward. "Ames, you and Fletcher check out the old line shack on Fletcher's land. Morrow and Heidelman will take the woods to the east, and Brandt and Sanders will start at the creek by the bridge and work their way north. I'll take the area near the cave. Any questions?"

Dandy stepped out into what was rapidly turning from drizzle to rain. He half-reared to express his opinion.

"What the hell—! Pardon, ma'am." One of the older men touched his hat to her, then scowled at Luke. "You can't mean to let that little lady ride out with us."

Maggie adjusted her reins. "The little lady makes her own decisions."

"And on one of those bitty little saddles, too." The man eyed Maggie's saddle with the deep distrust of a cowboy for English gear.

"Don't worry. Maggie can stick to that bitty saddle like she was glued to it. And she won't be riding out with you," Luke said, controlling Gotcha Girl's nervous sidling. "She's going with me."

"The land by the creek is all cut up," another man protested. "It's the roughest part of the search."

"Exactly. Maggie can cover rough ground faster than anyone here." Briefly his grin flashed. "Except me, of course."

She signaled Dandy to muscle his way through the other horses. They hadn't quite reached Luke when he wheeled Gotcha Girl's head around, dropped his hands—and off they went.

Dandy came to quivering alert, just as she'd known he would. She clasped him firmly, gave him one quick kick—and they took off into the night after Luke and Gotcha Girl.

My, oh my, that man could ride.

He didn't hold back on her account. He rode with every ounce of skill he possessed, coaxed every bit of speed he safely could from his mare—and a little more.

His skill surpassed hers. After fifteen minutes of hard riding, with the others well behind them, she had to admit that. She was keeping up, but only by watching him more than the ground they flew over, and matching her moves to his. And because Dandy, bless him, was hell-bent to catch the horse whose tail stayed just ahead, and a skilled and canny competitor on rough ground. She couldn't have done it on Gotcha Girl.

The fierce chase through the streaming rain thrilled her, and terrified her, in the odd moments when she allowed herself to notice. If she hadn't already been in love with Luke, she thought fleetingly as she and Dandy sailed over a downed tree she'd barely glimpsed in the rain-lashed darkness, she would have fallen for him tonight. Because he didn't cut her any slack.

Somewhere in the wildness of the ride, where there was room only for the quick, instinctive blur of motion and strain and instinct, the rain washed the last of her confusion from her. Everything she knew became clear.

If he thought she could do this, she would. Bending over Dandy's neck, she let him take the next stretch at a gallop. Because Luke was. And she trusted him—his skill, his judgment—and what he felt for her. She trusted him completely, because she trusted herself. Her instincts, her judgment—and what she'd sensed when he held her.

He'd given her that gift. Somehow, she would return it.

Then he was slowing. She eased Dandy from gallop to canter, coming up beside Gotcha Girl as both horses dropped to a walk. Somewhere nearby, unseen in the wet night, water rushed over rocks.

Luke looked at her as they came to a stop. Across the darkness, their eyes met.

Luke's heart was still galloping. He'd pushed himself, his horse—and Maggie. Pushed all of them faster than was safe, across rougher ground than anyone should ride at such a pace at night.

The rain frightened him.

There used to be two caves in the high, limestone banks that walled this section of the creek. One had collapsed two years ago. In the rain.

"The cave is below," he told her. "I'll have to go on foot. The drop-off is too steep for the horses." He swung down from Gotcha Girl's back. "I need you to stay with them."

"We can tie them," she said, dismounting.

"No." He hesitated. He hadn't wanted to frighten her, but if he didn't level with her now, she'd follow him. "The path to the cave is in bad shape. Crumbling. In this weather it will be unstable. The less weight on it, the better."

He heard her quick intake of breath. But she didn't argue, just nodded and reached for his reins.

He gave them to her, and moved off into the rain.

There was an easy path down to the creek, but it lay a mile to the south. He'd come directly to the section by the caves because the urgency clamoring in him wouldn't let up. Climbing down the bank in the dark, with the rock slippery and dirt crumbling beneath him, he wondered if he was risking his neck on a fool's errand. He couldn't know that Jeremy was here.

Yet he did. Every frantic beat of his heart urged him to hurry, hurry. Before it was too late.

When he landed on the narrow path next to the creek, the sound of the rushing water was loud. The creek was filling up. He peered ahead through the curtain of rain—and saw a light. Dim and unsteady, but a light.

Thank God.

His heart pounding, he followed the light through the straggle of brush. Then ducked beneath an earthen overhang, and stepped out of the rain.

The cave was about twelve feet deep. Jeremy sat on the sleeping bag at the back, arms huddled around bony knees for warmth. A big flashlight sat beside him. He glared at Luke. "I won't go back."

He wanted to drag the boy to safety and reason with him later. But some things, once broken, couldn't be fixed later. Acting on instinct, he ducked his head lower so he could join the boy, dropping down to sit next to him "Have you noticed the water that's running down that side of the cave?" he asked, nodding to his left. "That wall's likely to come down if it gets wet enough."

Jeremy's head swiveled left, then back. "It'll be okay."

"Maybe." Luke stretched out one leg, keeping an eye on the slick, wet earth to the left. "You ever done something stupid? I don't mean one-time stupid like holing up here, though that's plenty dumb. I'm talking about something you keep doing, over and over, because you don't know you're being stupid."

Jeremy didn't say anything. But he was watching Luke. And he was listening.

"I've been scared a time or two in my life," Luke admitted. "But never like I was tonight when I realized you were out here, alone. That you'd very likely come to the one place I'd forbidden you to go, and might be hurt. That you might very well get yourself killed, because I'd been stupid." He looked directly at Jeremy then. "Sometimes fear is good. It can wash out all the petty sh-stuff that messes up a man's thinking. I want you for my son, Jeremy.''

In the dim light Luke caught the sudden sheen of tears in the boy's eyes. And the way his fists clenched. ''You're a liar.''

Luke nodded. ''I'll let you get away with that this time. You've got reason to think it. I know what you overheard—me being stupid. And selfish. I thought I could go right on having you in my life part-time. I was afraid to want more. I was afraid of failing,'' he admitted softly. ''It was easier to have only a little of what I wanted than to try to have it all, and fail.''

''That's crap.'' But Jeremy sounded less certain this time.

''Yeah. But it's true crap. The kind that makes a man keep right on being stupid unless something shakes him out of it.'' He put a hand on one thin shoulder, and the boy didn't push him away. ''Jeremy. Come home with me. We'll sort it out—with the law, the courts. It may take a while, but—''

The earth bulged. Out of the corner of his eye, he saw it—up near the ceiling, the wet dirt swelled out like a bubble. He grabbed Jeremy and threw him toward the mouth of the cave, threw him free—just before the wall collapsed.

He rolled. Dirt fell on him, rocks, mud. He heard Jeremy cry out and the wet, slurping sound of mud moving. Then he came up against the boy's body, and shoved them both out into the rain.

The light was gone. The earth was still again, and somehow he was on his feet, Jeremy's arms around him, his thin body shaking. Rain poured down over them both. There was a trickle of warmth on his face he knew must be blood.

He raised a shaking hand and smoothed the boy's wet

hair and held him. Just held on tight. "It's all right. Everything will be all right now."

The rain had ended. The house was quiet when Luke came back inside after seeing off the last of the neighbors. Jeremy had been hugged, cried over, scolded and fed hot chocolate by the women, and was safe in bed now. Jacob and Claire were in one of the spare bedrooms; Sarita was in another.

And Maggie? he thought. Where was she? Not in the living room or the den, he discovered. And not, he learned with heartfelt relief, in the bedroom she'd used when she first came to his house.

He'd finished the first course of the night's challenges. He had another tough hurdle ahead. But at least she was in the bedroom they'd come to share.

It gave him hope. He pushed open the door and saw her standing in front of the window. The blinds were open fully, and the dark sky, ablaze with stars, framed her quiet figure.

She was wearing an orange sweatshirt and saggy blue sweatpants. He smiled. Much as he loved her in satin and lace, she was so very much herself in the old sweats.

Maggie turned. There was something in her face he couldn't read, something that made the clutch of anxiety tighten in his chest. "We need to talk."

"Yes." He closed the door behind him. "We do."

She took a deep breath. "You should know that I've changed my mind."

He froze.

"I know we agreed to divorce when the trust is settled. I'm not planning on letting you do that, Luke." She started toward him. "I'll fight you on this if I have to." She stopped in front of him, her chin tilted belligerently. "Don't make me get rough."

His breath whooshed out. Joy rushed in. "Okay, I

won't. Maggie.'' He cupped her face in both hands and spoke with every bit of truth in him. ''I love you.''

A tremor went through her. Those beautiful eyes filled. And she sniffed. ''Luke. Oh, Luke, I love you so much. I thought I'd never be able to say it.'' Her arms came around him and his were around her, and she was laughing. Or maybe crying. ''I knew you cared. I was almost sure you loved me, but I didn't think you knew it. Or that you'd admit it.''

''I tried my best not to. God.'' He rubbed his face on her hair, breathing in the scent of her, filling himself up with the feel of her. ''I've been a fool for such a long time.''

She nodded firmly. ''Damn right you have.''

Her ready—and profane—agreement made him chuckle, but humor faltered in sudden uncertainty. ''I don't see how you can trust me.''

''You will.'' She leaned back in his arms and blessed him with a smile so shining he felt it all the way down. ''I do trust you, Luke. You'll get to where you do, too.''

''I've still got a lot to sort out.''

''You'll get there,'' she said again, snuggling her head against his shoulder. ''We've got time.''

Time. It was a precious gift, almost as precious as the trust she handed him so freely, along with her heart. Luke knew the important things now; he could take his time figuring out the thoughts that went with what he felt, what he knew in his heart.

Jacob had given him a nudge in the right direction. All his life, Luke had found distance and safety in numbers, just as Jacob had isolated himself behind those chilly walls of his. Just as Michael had always chased after danger, as if risking his life was safer than living it. There was more, a jumble of impressions he didn't fully understand—his feelings about his mother, a fear of jealousy. He'd buried that one deep, he thought, had fashioned a lifestyle to keep him safe from that particular brand of madness. Or so he'd believed.

Until his brother started seeing Maggie, and all his carefully constructed walls began to crumble. He didn't know exactly how it had happened, or why one woman out of so many became *the* woman. The only one who mattered.

Maggie's fingers crept up under his shirt, teased the waist of his pants. "I think I'm ready for another lesson," she said. "Only this time, I get to be the rider."

He laughed and swept her up into his arms. "We'll take turns," he told her, smiling down into her glowing eyes.

Perhaps love was always a mystery. Luke only knew that the woman in his arms was Maggie. *His* Maggie. And that made all the difference.

*   *   *   *   *

*There's one more West wedding
before the trust is broke.
Look out for MICHAEL'S TEMPTATION
(SD1409)
coming next month—only from
Silhouette Desire!*

CALL THE ONES YOU LOVE OVER THE HOLIDAYS!

Save $25 off future book purchases when you buy any four Harlequin® or Silhouette® books in October, November and December 2001,

PLUS

receive a phone card good for 15 minutes of long-distance calls to anyone you want in North America!

WHAT AN INCREDIBLE DEAL!

Just fill out this form and attach 4 proofs of purchase (cash register receipts) from October, November and December 2001 books, and Harlequin Books will send you a coupon booklet worth a total savings of $25 off future purchases of Harlequin® and Silhouette® books, AND a 15-minute phone card to call the ones you love, anywhere in North America.

Please send this form, along with your cash register receipts as proofs of purchase, to:
In the USA: Harlequin Books, P.O. Box 9057, Buffalo, NY 14269-9057
In Canada: Harlequin Books, P.O. Box 622, Fort Erie, Ontario L2A 5X3
Cash register receipts must be dated no later than December 31, 2001.
Limit of 1 coupon booklet and phone card per household.
Please allow 4-6 weeks for delivery.

I accept your offer! Enclosed are 4 proofs of purchase.
Please send me my coupon booklet
and a 15-minute phone card:

Name: _____

Address: _____ City: _____

State/Prov.: _____ Zip/Postal Code: _____

Account Number (if available): _____

---

097 KJB DAGL
PHQ4013

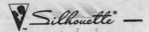